JESUS HAD A NEAR-DEATH EXPERIENCE

A NOVEL BY

RONALD C. MEYER

AND

MARK REEDER

HANGAR 1 PUBLISHING

© 2024 by Ronald C. Meyer and Mark Reeder

First Edition. All rights reserved

All rights reserved. No part of this book may be reproduced, stored or transmitted in any form or by any means—whether auditory, graphic, mechanical or electronic—without written permission of the author, except in the case of brief excerpts used in critical articles and reviews. Unauthorized reproduction of any part of this work is illegal and is punishable by law.

This is a work of fiction. All of the characters, names, incidents, organizations and dialogue in this novel are either products of the author's imagination or are used fictitiously.

ACKNOWLEDGMENTS

We would like to thank our amazing editor Kelly Lynne Schaub who made this novel come together.

OTHER BOOKS BY RON MEYER AND MARK REEDER

Center: The Power of Aikido

Tricksters and Angels

Simulation

Aliens 2035

The High Strangeness of Bradshaw Ranch

The Bigfoot Alien Connection Revisited

Young Adult Books

The Adventures of Andrew Raymond

The Crystal Sword Series

Book 1: A Dark Knight for the King

Book 2: Queen's Knight Gambit

Book 3: Knight to Mate

Other Books by Ron Meyer

Aikido in America

Extinction

18 and a Half Minutes

Other Books by Mark Reeder

Where Memory Has Lease

Shadowloom Series

Shadowloom

Weft of the Universe

Jack Doyle Series

Astral: A Jack Doyle Paranormal Mystery

Nagual: Jack Doyle Returns

Daemon: Jack Doyle on the Edge

Young Adult Books by Mark Reeder

Marc Holiday Series

Marc Holiday and the Sand Reckoner - 1

Marc Holiday and the Travelers Ring - 2

Marc Holiday and the Curious Cusp of Time – 3

Marc Holiday and the Moons of Ararat – 4

Marc Holiday and the Dragon's Eye – 5

Earth Upheaval Series

Imp – 1

PROLOGUE

EARLY FIRST CENTURY AD.
JUDAEAN DESERT

A young man with the name Yeshua came to John the Baptist and asked to be baptized. The prophet, following the teachings of the Essenes at the Qumran Monastery, lowered Yeshua into the Jordan River. When the young man was lifted from the water, a glow fell about him. Many in the crowd bowed. Yeshua, humbled by the experience, asked the prophet, "What shall I do?"

John placed a hand on the young man's head and said, "You will find the answers to your questions in the Judaean Desert. You must go alone, eat no food, and drink only the water that the land provides."

Yeshua thanked the prophet and left the banks of the Jordan River for the harshness of the desert.

For twelve days Yeshua wandered in the wilderness. He cast aside the temptations to return to his gentler and richer life as the son of a carpenter. On the thirteenth day, weak from hunger and little water, he fell to the ground and cried. The heat bore down on him, and he wondered if God had forsaken him.

But a gentle hand lifted him up. A beautiful woman with the name Mary took him by the hand and led them to the entrance of a nearby cave. There they met a man in strange garments.

Yeshua asked, "Who are you?"

The mysterious stranger answered, "I am Mary's guide and perhaps yours."

Lack of food and water clouded Yeshua's mind, but not so much he didn't recognize he was being tested. "Go on."

The strangely dressed man smiled. "I have three questions to ask you. First, if you are the son of God, turn these stones into bread so we may eat and be full."

Yeshua smiled back, for this was a simple puzzle and he knew the answer, even if he was starving. "It is written that man does not live by bread alone."

The stranger nodded. "If thou be the son of God, cast thyself down from the temple at Jerusalem: for it is written, 'He shall give his angels charge over thee, to keep thee, and in their hands, they shall bear thee up, lest at any time thou dash thy foot against a stone.'"

Again, Yeshua knew he was being tempted to prove his oneness with God, but he shook his head. "It is written thou shall not tempt the Lord thy God."

Once more the stranger smiled. He swept his hand across the rock face of the cave and pictures appeared. In these pictures, Yeshua saw the kingdoms of the world from Rome in the west to India and China in the east.

The stranger declared, "All these things I will give you if you fall down and do an act of worship to me."

Yeshua stood and cried out, "It is written: 'You shall worship the Lord your God and only Him shall you serve.'"

The test taxed Yeshua, and he might have fallen, so weak was he from lack of food and water, but Mary caught his arm and helped him to sit. She and the mysterious stranger smiled down at him.

"Welcome, Yeshua," the strangely dressed guide said.

Yeshua asked, "What are those strange garments?"

The man replied, "They are from the future, from a people who also live in a desert, though different from this one, and search also for what you are seeking."

The guide waved his hand again, and the cave became illuminated. Greek symbols were etched on the walls. Yeshua recognized them from his teachings as the fundamental sounds of language and consciousness. The guide began a chant and Mary joined in, beckoning Yeshua to add his voice. The chant emptied his mind.

In the silence that followed, the guide gave Yeshua a substance to consume then held up a Greek votive stone known as the Eye. Yeshua stared into the Eye, and the universe opened to him. Gentle hands laid him upon the floor of the cave.

For a period of time, his body lay motionless as if he were dead on the rocky cave floor. When he awakened, he said, "I understand now; I died, and I have been reborn. I am the son of God just as all of us are God's children and at the same time the same as me." This is what Yeshua would preach to those who would listen. He was rich with new powers and capable of miracles.

Mary and Yeshua, now united in a new heavenly love, stood before the guide. He blessed them both, and taking up a pen and papyrus rolled into a large scroll, he said, "I shall record all that has happened."

Two thousand years later, in 1947, the ancient scroll and Greek votive stone Eye were discovered in the mystery cave.

1

BEGINNINGS

LAS VEGAS, NEVADA

Sarah Davenport navigated the labyrinth of people and dazzling displays at the Las Vegas Convention Center immersed in the kaleidoscopic world of the Consumer Electronics Show. Every January, tech titans and visionary thinkers gathered at the turn of the new year to unveil the future. For Sarah, this was more than an ordinary commercial event—this place stirred haunting memories.

Ten years ago, Sarah walked these halls with her father, Simon Ravensbach, shortly after her seventeenth birthday. He ran a booth promoting his revolutionary company, Psi-Vision, which used virtual reality to evoke transcendent experiences akin to moderate doses of psychedelics like LSD and psilocybin. The technology promised to unlock mystical states of consciousness, leading to profound self-discovery. Her father hoped she would follow in his footsteps, crafting the next generation of technological marvels. But something deeper drew Sarah's heart—she was more concerned with the well-being of people than pushing the boundaries of innovation.

Now, a decade later, the Psi-Vision booth loomed ahead, three times the size Sarah remembered. Her phone buzzed in her hand, pulling her back to the present. A flash of panic hit her—only ten minutes left until she was due backstage. She moved through the crowd with purpose, quickening her pace.

As she reached the expansive hallway leading to the convention's enormous auditorium, the crowd thickened, hundreds of attendees lining up for the awards ceremony honoring her father. Picking up speed, she jogged toward the backstage entrance, where a security guard checked her ID before ushering her inside. Sarah slipped through a maze of curtains and found herself in the opulent embrace of the green room, a sanctuary of calm before the storm.

The lavish surroundings, from the deep crimson carpet to the gaudy overstuffed sofas and fully stocked mini bar, dwarfed her presence. The room overflowed with extravagance, offering a feast for the senses with elaborate canapés, expensive wines, and sophisticated coffees. Sarah couldn't help but clench her teeth at the sight of such wastefulness.

She turned away, eyes drawn to three massive screens broadcasting world news, while a smaller one showcased the charismatic emcee of tonight's awards ceremony, entertaining the lavishly dressed crowd before unveiling the recipient of the prestigious Robert Bigelow Space and Aeronautics Achievement Prize.

Across from Sarah, her father appeared unperturbed, his eyes closed as if in deep meditation. Oblivious to the ostentatious display intended to honor his greatness, a subtle, mocking smile played upon his thin lips. He found comfort in knowing his real achievement wasn't in accolades, but in how his work advanced the field of Astronautics.

The screens shifted to an advertisement for the upcoming Women's Winter Cup Gymnastics competition, the first step in being selected for the Olympic team. Simon, opening his eyes for the first time since Sarah rushed into the room, glanced at the gymnasts and casually remarked, "That could have been you."

The words stung, reminding her of the injury that crushed her childhood Olympic dreams. A broken ankle sidelined her just as she reached her competitive peak. She narrowed her eyes and crossed her arms. Her dad had never supported her Olympic ambitions. "I always wondered why you left everything to Mom and the trainers you hired."

"You needed social normalcy and a way to develop your super-human physical capabilities. Someday, I hope to tell you why I kept so distant."

She was about to ask what he meant when a precognitive moment, a vision of the future, took over her mind's eye as if on cue. They came to her as though from a separate source, like her mind was catching a satellite signal from beyond and commanded her complete attention. Sarah had experienced many of these second-sighted events over the course of her life and knew how to let them run their course.

In this one, she saw herself with a man unknown to her, entering a cave. The walls of the cave shimmered, adorned with strange, glowing symbols. The two of them sat across from one another, their voices weaving a chant that echoed through the darkness. And then, as with so many of these visions, the cave, the symbols, and the mysterious man dissolved into a blinding light.

Simon recognized that his daughter had moved into an altered state but had seldom witnessed it play out before. He waited calmly for the visionary interlude to end. The glazed look in Sarah's eyes faded, replaced by an intense brightness as if she had experienced a satori moment. "Welcome back," he said.

She caught her father staring at her and nodded. She might have said more, but the sound from the television screens fell silent, show-casing the emcee, poised at the dais, commencing his introduction of the visionary Simon Ravensbach and the remarkable achievements that earned him the esteemed Bigelow Aeronautics Prize, second only to the Nobel in prominence.

"Greater than a Nobel," her father quipped, winking at her.

Sarah returned his smile. "Do you have your speech ready?"

Simon patted his coat pocket, retrieving a three-by-five note card filled with his barely decipherable scrawl.

"That's it?" Sarah chuckled, amused at the paucity of his speech.

"Brevity befits greatness—"

"And captivates the crowd," Sarah interjected, completing his sentence.

"That's my girl."

Curiosity sparked within Sarah as she questioned her father's motive for summoning her backstage. "Why did you want me back here with you?"

Simon's lips pursed momentarily, erasing the smile from his face. "It's quieter back here."

"Quieter?" Sarah's keen ears detected a hint of uncertainty in her father's usually composed tone.

"You never know who's in a crowd like that. Besides, we can retreat to my room at the hotel and enjoy a meal worthy of the name," he remarked dismissively, gesturing disdainfully at the trays of party food provided by the Convention Center.

She followed her father's restless glance toward both entrances to the green room, one from the hall, the other from the stage, sensing his unease. "What's wrong, Dad?"

He smiled and shook his head, dismissing her misgivings. With a reassuring nod, he uttered, "Nothing. We're safe here. Ezekiel is guarding the door."

Ezekiel Simmons, professionally known as Simon Ravensbach's bodyguard and gopher, held a far more significant role in their lives than that. He was Simon's confidant and right-hand man, instrumental in realizing the ambitious projects undertaken by the Ravensbach Creative Technology Group. Simon had often emphasized to Sarah the indispensable role of Ezekiel in bringing the Group's ideas to the marketplace.

The sudden disruption of a jarring crash near the green room's hall entrance startled both. With the agility of a cat, Simon sprang out of his seat and swiftly made his way toward the stage entrance. His rapid movements defied his sixty-three years. As he reached the midpoint of the room, the curtains parted, revealing a figure clad in a black robe and wearing a golden mask resembling common depictions of Jesus of Nazareth.

Without hesitation, the masked intruder brandished a pistol with sound suppressor and squeezed the trigger twice. The suppressed crack of each round exploded in Sarah's ears. The sight of her father collapsing onto the carpet sent shockwaves through her being. Standing over him, the assailant aimed the gun at his head.

Without thinking, Sarah hurled the Perrier bottle at the intruder, striking his wrist. The impact caused the pistol to spin out of his grasp, disappearing behind the sofa her father occupied only moments ago. The golden Jesus face fixed on her, its radiant brilliance masking the malevolence of the person hiding behind it. Sarah hardly dared breathe.

A stage attendant called out from the stage entrance, "We're ready for you, Dr. Ravensbach."

"Sic Semper Tyrannis," the assailant said before running from the room the way he had come.

Sarah moved to pursue him, but her father's strained voice stopped her. "Sarah... no."

She sank to her knees beside him. "Daddy..." Her gaze fell upon the two crimson stains on his chest, and her speech dissolved into anguished sobs. Desperately rummaging through her jeans pockets, she retrieved her cell phone to call 911.

"There's no time, Sarah," her father whispered hoarsely. "Listen carefully. We've been betrayed. You must escape. Remember these numbers... 1162413. Call General Deke Davidson—" His voice trailed off, and his eyes glazed over.

The stage attendant entered the room. "Dr. Ravensbach?" She stopped, eyes widening at the bloody scene before her.

Though deep down she knew it was too late, Sarah said, "Call an ambulance."

Watching the young girl punch 911 into her phone, Sarah was already contemplating her next move. *You have to get out of here,* she commanded herself. Her father's last words "we've been betrayed" made that clear. The precog part of her mind confirmed she couldn't be here when the police arrived. They'd ask too many questions. She had no doubt the man who shot her father was like her, special, a mutant.

The attendant ran back onto the stage.

Sarah stood, her world shattered in an instant. Her father had been gunned down right in front of her eyes, and now, every beat of her heart echoed the shot that killed him. Numb and on autopilot, she walked out of the green room, her movements mechanical, as if her body knew what to do even when her mind couldn't. The corridor stretched before her like a tunnel of confusion, leading her back into the buzzing sea of the exhibition floor. People swarmed around her, oblivious to the storm raging inside her. She pushed through the crowd, her focus solely on the exit, her thoughts tangled in a haze of shock and dread.

She collided with a young man—red hair, big grin—who seemed completely out of place in her dark reality. "Sorry. I slipped," she muttered, her voice distant as she dropped her cell phone into his bag, an action so casual it barely registered. She didn't wait for a response, her feet carrying her outside, where the world spun on as if nothing had changed. The colorful tents of the media companies felt like a surreal carnival, but Sarah had no time to dwell on them. Her instincts, sharpened by panic, guided her through the chaos toward the lane where buses idled, ready to whisk people back to their hotels.

She scanned the buses, waiting for the right moment. When she saw one about to pull away, she bolted toward it, her legs moving with a speed born of desperation. "Hold up!" she shouted, her voice cutting through the noise. The door hissed open, and she climbed aboard, slipping into a seat as if it could shield her from the reality crashing down around her.

Once settled, the flood of grief she had been holding at bay came rushing in. Tears blurred her vision, and she buried her head in her hands, her father's final moments replaying in her mind, over and over, like a nightmare she couldn't wake from. Grief turned to anger, and from that anger, a terrible thought surfaced, dark and cold. The people who had sent the assassin to murder her father wouldn't stop. They wouldn't rest. They would come for her.

2

ISAAC JOHNS
TEMPE, ARIZONA

Dr. Isaac Johns, a renowned Yale scholar of ancient Roman and Greek mysteries, sat at his desk early this Saturday morning amidst a sea of scattered notes and aged texts, preparing for his guest lectures at Arizona State University. Drawn window shades blocked out the bright September sun, allowing only two slivers of light to intersect on his immaculate desk, creating an eerie cross at its center. The beams of light fell upon a picture frame as though X marked the spot. Johns smiled at the picture of his wife, Helene, and then dragged his focus back to the subject of Monday's seminar—the influence of Greek Gods in everyday Athenian life, a topic that had formed his successful academic career. This was the first lecture for a new book he was writing, and he wanted everything to go perfectly. His difficulty was in scaling his wealth of knowledge on the subject down to a basic, introductory class.

The shrill ring of his phone broke his concentration. The Facetime notification revealed the ID of his former Princeton roommate, Zack Helm, a filmmaker. Though their fields of study differed, the two men had forged a bond through esoteric martial arts and a shared fascination with the arcane.

Johns chuckled and tapped "answer."

Zack's familiar face filled the tiny screen. Sandy hair now thinning, a few more lines etched onto his narrow cheeks since they last met a couple of years ago, Zack possessed an air of rugged resilience.

"You look like crap, Isaac," Zack teased, his gray eyes sharp as ever.

"I was up most of the night. I get to deliver a lecture on Monday morning on the role of Mount Olympus in Greek daily life."

"Some people have all the luck." Zack paused before a smile split his face.

"What's got you grinning like a Cheshire cat?"

"It's something big... urgent, man," Zack's voice crackled with excitement. "A project that has all the hallmarks of a blockbuster documentary series ... secret locations ... journeys to the mystical landscapes, like Sedona ... Native American shamans ... and best of all, we'll be blindfolded."

"You writing a script for a movie?" Johns asked, amused by his friend's intensity. It reminded him of their youthful daydreams of making a major archaeological discovery like Indiana Jones.

"It's the real deal, Isaac."

"And when are we supposed to do all this?"

"We leave this afternoon with—"

"Today?" Johns interrupted. "Where the hell are you?"

"In Phoenix."

Zack was here in town? The suddenness of the plan took him aback. "Whoa, old friend. No can do. I'm lecturing this semester at ASU, and—"

"When does the class start?"

"Monday."

"Then you're golden. Our odyssey will only take today."

Johns hesitated, contemplating his current commitments. "I understand your excitement, Zack, but I have responsibilities I can't simply abandon."

Zack's expression turned serious. "Isaac, I wouldn't ask if it wasn't important. This could launch me into the big time as a serious documentary filmmaker. Plus, the person funding me insists on having you along, otherwise, it's no deal."

This aroused Johns' curiosity but also his caution. Why would anyone insist on his participation? He was a scholar who combed through archives, not a digger unearthing relics of the past. Sure, he was in shape and loved the desert southwest, but—

He took a deep breath. "Why me?"

"One word: Eleusinian."

Johns' heart skipped a beat. For a moment, he couldn't speak. The Eleusinian Mysteries had captivated him the moment he visited the ruins north of Athens. There, for nearly two millennia, from around 1600 BCE to 392 CE, devotees held ancient religious rites in honor of the goddess Demeter and her daughter Persephone. Johns' studies ever since suggested these mystery practices were among the most significant in ancient Greece.

Sweat broke out on Johns' forehead. "Christ, is this for real?"

"Yes, supposedly there are Greek inscriptions relating to the mysteries in a cave."

Johns wrestled with conflicting emotions, torn between his commitments and the potential knowledge he could gain. The central theme of the Eleusinian Mysteries revolved around the cycle of life and death, and the promise of rebirth and eternal life. The rites were closely guarded secrets, and initiates were sworn to silence about the details of the ceremonies. To have that kind of knowledge was something Johns' academic heart longed for.

He let out the breath he'd been holding. "Alright. Count me in."

Zack Helm's face lit up like a little boy's at Christmas. "Perfect. As I said, the whole trip will only take a few hours. By tonight, we'll be kicking back in Tempe, drinking beers ... maybe hit a jazz show in Phoenix. I'll pick you up at noon. Oh, do you have a daypack?"

"Just a briefcase."

"Go buy one. There's a Dick's Sporting Goods near the ASU campus. You'll need it for water and food. Also, I need you to schlep some camera gear for me."

"Camera gear? Do I need a big pack?"

"Nah. The gear is packed and ready." Zack hit end call, and Johns' cell phone screen reverted to the picture of him and his wife on their wedding day. He shook his head ruefully. *Helene would have said yes in a heartbeat.*

The Eleusinian Mysteries, a tantalizing enigma of life, death, and rebirth, had eluded complete understanding for two thousand years. The possibility of their resurgence in North America bewildered as much as thrilled him. Johns pounded the desk. Papers scattered. Hastily, he picked them up and rearranged them.

As the initial excitement faded, doubts assailed Johns. He threshed his graying hair. Though physically fit, the invitation to adventure in Arizona's desert southwest made him feel like a fish in a tree. Whoever heard of Greek mystery schools in North America? The notion was as preposterous as turning lead into gold.

Johns picked up his phone, intending to call Zack back and let him know he couldn't possibly make it. His finger hesitated over the call button. His thoughts flashed to what Cicero had said about the Eleusinian Mysteries: "For among the many excellent and indeed divine institutions which your Athens has brought forth and contributed to human life, none, in my opinion, is better than those mysteries. For by means of them we have been brought out of our barbarous and savage mode of life and educated and refined to a state of civilization; and as the rites are called 'initiations,' so in very truth we have learned from them the beginnings of life and have gained the power not only to live happily but also to die with a better hope."

"What if the Eleusinian Mystery Schools have been resurrected here in Arizona?" Johns whispered to himself. Putting the phone down, he went to the window and threw back the drapes. Sunlight flooded the office. He gazed upon the Superstition Mountains. "It's only a day," he thought.

3

THE ACCIDENT

PHOENIX

Isaac Johns parked his Toyota Prius under the meager shade of an old, gnarled olive tree, the only respite from the sweltering heat in the mall's sprawling parking lot. Black spots from the dark fruit stained the asphalt. Consulting his phone's map app, he noted Dick's Sporting Goods as the nearest camping equipment supplier.

Johns locked the doors and headed across the blistering asphalt. Late September in Phoenix mocked the fall season, the temperature stubbornly hovering at a hundred even in the shade. *Damn, but I miss New England.* His mind wandered to the vivid fall colors of Connecticut's forests and the invigorating, crisp air that cleansed one's lungs with the spirit of autumn.

Inevitably, his thoughts wandered to Helene. Autumn in New England was their favorite time of year. Amidst the rustic charm of the Mystic Seaport Museum, she proposed to him on October fourteenth, capping off a whirlwind courtship that blossomed in Rome. He had been leading a National Geographic tour of the Eternal City's sacred sites when her deep, metaphysical questions, delivered in a warm southern drawl, caught his attention. Helene, fresh from earning her PhD in philosophy from Rice University, explored the intersections of phenomenology and Alan Watt's teachings in her doctoral thesis. They spent the rest of the tour together, and later when he returned to the states, he discovered she lived in New Haven, where he would begin teaching in the fall.

They married the following autumn. Fourteen more years passed since those idyllic days. Helene found success in New York City as a book editor and a pioneering podcaster. Her motto, "the blind shall finally see"—a nod to Plato's allegory of the cave—became synonymous with her insightful approach.

Johns' brow creased as the memory threatened to pull him back to the day of Helene's accident one year ago. With a Herculean effort, he warded off the despairing spiral of reliving her last hours in the hospital. He refocused on the present, on the shopping list Zack had texted—a daypack for bottled water, trail mix, and ten candy bars. He smiled; Zack's penchant for calling candy bars "field rations" never failed to amuse him. Despite his sweet tooth, Zack maintained his health, defying logic.

Doors whooshed open and Johns walked gratefully into the air-conditioned comfort of the sporting goods store. Large signs above the aisles advertised various products. He headed for the outdoor camping gear. On the way he passed by a rack of books. He glanced at the titles: Ansel Adams, *Yosemite and the Range of Light*; John Muir, *My First Summer in the Sierra*; Henry David Thoreau, *On Walden Pond*. *Woman and Nature* by Helene Durham, his wife's final book, caught his eye. Abruptly he stopped, narrowly avoiding a woman pushing a shopping cart behind him.

"I'm ... I'm sorry," Johns stammered. His head hurt and the strength drained from his legs. He leaned against the rack and stared helplessly at a book on the top row—a collection of talks from his wife's highly successful podcast *Into the Unknown*.

He pulled the book from the rack. Helene's photo dominated the back cover. Dark hair framed a narrow face with a prominent nose above thin lips and a strong chin. Her amber eyes and burnished copper skin complemented a Mona Lisa smile. Rather than a professional head shot, she had insisted on using the snapshot he took with his phone on their last wedding anniversary, mere weeks before the book's release and her tragic bicycle accident. He swallowed hard. Helpless against the tidal wave of memories crashing over him, he drowned again in the last day of Helene's life.

* * *

The shrill sound of a phone cut through the quiet atmosphere of Yale's SLB Lecture Hall. Johns looked up from his notes. "Whose phone—" He stopped as he realized it was his; he had forgotten to mute it. He glanced at the caller ID and his heart clenched—Yale New Haven Hospital. "That'll be all," he said, abruptly ending the class.

Students looked around, puzzled. The lecture had fifteen minutes to go. A few filed down the steps toward the podium.

Johns stared dumbfounded at the caller ID, which blazed like an alarm on the screen. He waved them away and answered the call.

"Dr. Johns?" a sympathetic voice asked.

He swallowed hard against the fear filling his body "Yes."

"I'm calling from Yale New Haven Hospital. I'm sorry to tell you your wife has been in an accident. She's in the emergency room."

Johns rushed out of the lecture hall. At the hospital's ER, he tried to bull his way past the admitting desk into the emergency area. The security guard stopped him, big hands gripping both shoulders with incredible softness. "Sir, I'm sorry. You can't go back there unless you've checked in at the desk."

Johns fell against him. "My wife ... where is she?" he pleaded, tears threatening to spill. The guard led him to the admitting desk and told the woman who Johns was here to see. She got up to go check, and the guard helped Johns to a seat in the waiting area. "Someone will come out to get you soon," the young man said before returning to his post.

An hour passed. People came into the ER, waited in line at the admitting desk to check in, and were directed to sit and wait for triage. Periodically, a nurse would come out from the back and call a name, but never his.

At last, someone called his name. Johns leapt from his seat and hurried over to her. The dark-haired woman with wire-rimmed glasses was much shorter than him. She looked up with kind eyes. "Dr. Johns, please follow me." She guided him to a glass-walled isolation room in the back of the ER. "I'm sorry," she said and left him.

On the other side of the glass door, his wife lay inert on the hospital bed hooked to a ventilator, a monitor with bright green lines on it, and several IVs. Doctors and nurses had done their best to cover up the worst of the accident, but there was no denying Helene's condition. She looked impossibly small, as though much of the life had been sucked out of her, leaving a shrunken frame where a vibrant woman had once been. Machines on either side of the bed whirred and beeped, the displays with abbreviated medial jargon and numbers a mystery.

The following hours blurred as Helene was transferred to the ICU. Time and visiting hours lost their meaning as Johns sat by her side, constantly talking to her, aware that hearing was the last sense to go.

A slight, young Asian man in scrubs entered the room. His ID tag was flipped backward, furthering Johns' impression that the medical staff were all anonymous drones. "Dr. Johns, I'm from the organ procurement organization. We're terribly sorry for your loss."

"Helene's not dead," Johns replied, his voice tight with defiance.

The doctor, or whatever he was, typed notes into the computer on the rolling stand nearby. "Sir, Helene will never wake up. Her heart is being artificially supported to keep her organs going, but her brain has ceased all activity." He showed Johns the EEG reading and explained what the display indicated.

Johns gripped Helene's hand tighter and willed her to speak, to prove the doctors wrong. But she remained still, her head wrapped in bandages, eyes closed like a lifeless statue.

"Dr.—"

"It's Isaac," Johns interrupted sharply.

"Yes, sir. According to her medical records, Helene had a living will and wished to become an organ donor. Her decision will help many people."

The words washed over him, but anger surged. His fists clenched, and he stood abruptly, towering over the small physician. He opened his mouth, ready to shout, "GET OUT!" But his voice caught in his throat.

His vision shifted as if seeing into another world. Without warning, his awareness split. In that moment, Johns saw his wife without any of the accident trauma, as beautiful as ever.

Helene opened her eyes. Her soft southern voice filled the room. "Oh wow, I'm free. It'll be okay. The distance between you and me is razor thin—so close to joining me."

"Helene," Johns whispered, voice cracking.

She moved as if to embrace him, but her body fell back to the bed. Her love enveloped him, deeper than words could express. His heart soared and shattered at once.

As her eyes closed again, her radiant presence faded.

The OPO doctor turned to Johns. "Are you okay?" he asked, concern in his eyes.

Johns blinked, his ordinary awareness snapping back into focus. His wife's bandaged body lay limp on the bed, an empty shell, though the machines were technically keeping her body alive. "Did you see her?" he asked, breathless.

"What are you talking about?"

"My wife... she..." Johns stopped, realization dawning. Helene had come to him—briefly, powerfully—to reassure him. To tell him everything would be alright. He placed a hand on Helene's cooling arm. "It's okay. Helene is at peace. She's where she wants to be."

He took a deep breath, accepting the enormity of it. Helene had chosen not to return. Leaning down, he kissed her softly on the lips. "Goodbye, sweetheart."

He turned to the doctor, his voice serene. "She would like helping others. Please, harvest whatever you can. That's the term, right?" Johns looked at her one last time, remembering her loving, radiant smile.

In the months following her death, Johns dove into research on near-death experiences, searching for answers. He needed to understand her final moment—why she chose to leave this realm and why he had been granted that extraordinary, shared glimpse into it. The question of why she had to die still haunted him, but he carried with him the peace of knowing death was not final.

Johns squeezed his eyes tight. The memory faded. Back in the present, he pushed away from the book rack. He gently touched the book cover, his fingers brushing Helene's image. He turned toward the rear of the store. Willing himself not to look back, he concentrated on Zack's list. "Daypack first," he muttered.

4

THE SON
SEDONA, ARIZONA

One hundred twenty miles north of Phoenix, Janus Snyder sat in a room off the Sedona regional airport's baggage claim area. He had on khaki pants, a light blue cotton shirt, and well-worn hiking boots. Around his neck he wore a silver medallion with the image of the Greek God Dionysus, son of Zeus, on one side and the crucifix on the other. He had hazel eyes, a cleft chin and full lips. A thin white line angled across his brow and disappeared into his receding blond hair. The scar was a constant reminder of his last tour of duty in Basra.

Beside Snyder, his companion animal, Turk, waited patiently. The Dutch shepherd had been trained for use in the *Nederlandse krijgsmacht*, the Netherlands Armed Forces. When Snyder had ended his tour of duty in the *Koninklijke Luchtmacht*, the Royal Netherlands Air Force, he adopted the dog. They traveled everywhere together.

The white-walled room was stark. A bare overhead bulb cast sharp light upon a single chair and a small writing desk on a concrete floor. A single window overlooked the helipad, where a Bell Long-Ranger 206 copter waited, blades twirling lazily in Arizona's high desert heat.

After a knock on the door, a young man yelled out, "The copter is ready."

Snyder suppressed his eagerness, reminding himself of the importance of ritual. *All must proceed in the correct manner, or else failure will be the only answer.* "I need a few more minutes," he called out.

The young man answered, "It's your chopper."

Once alone, Snyder opened the tan canvas bag at his feet. Turk whined and lifted his gray and black head. His large pink tongue licked his canine teeth twice. Snyder gave him a treat and thumped his strong flank. "We'll be leaving soon, boy."

Delving deeper into the bag, Snyder retrieved a golden mask molded in the likeness of the Christian Messiah, Jesus. The iconic mask fit seamlessly to his features. Clasping the mask in both hands, he chanted a Gnostic prayer seeking divine communion in the same manner Jesus would have prayed to the Father of All. The ancient rite, steeped in mystery, still held power for him, despite his departure from the Gnostics' core teachings.

Gnosticism, at its heart, was about "gnosis" – a profound, mystical knowledge of a higher power, transcending the material world and accessible only to the initiated. Gnostic cosmogony distinguished between a supreme God, hidden from humanity, and a malevolent divinity who created the material universe. As a result, Gnostics considered material existence flawed and believed the only way to achieve salvation was direct knowledge of the hidden god, attained via mystical or esoteric insight. Gnostic teachings dealt not in the Christian concepts of sin and repentance, but union with the divine.

Once he completed the prayer, Snyder's heart raced with anticipation. *Soon I will find the new site of the Eleusinian Mystery School. The next step in the Cleanse will be complete.* He worked hard to contain his fervor, striving to maintain a clear heart and neutral spirit. "Open up to emptiness, and miracles shall follow," he whispered to himself, reflecting on his liberation from his parents' oppressive Invisibles Academy upbringing.

He put away the golden mask of the Christian Messiah and

zipped up the bag. His phone rang. Snyder recognized the voice of his contact. "Yes, sir."

"Sarah has left Phoenix. She has Zack Helm and Dr. Isaac Johns with her," the man said.

Snyder drew in a sharp breath at the name. Johns was the key. "Excellent, sir."

"You know what to do."

Snyder's second bag beside the canvas tote held a Heckler & Koch G28 sniper rifle using 7.62 mm x 51 NATO rounds. "Copy that," he affirmed, ready for what was to come.

The call ended. Picking up both bags, Snyder left the room. Turk followed obediently at his heels. He strode toward the helicopter, his resolve as unwavering as his stride.

5

SARAH
TEMPE, ARIZONA

Sarah Davenport sat alone outside on the Kranzler Café's patio sipping iced coffee with a splash of vanilla syrup. The hot, late-September air had sent other patrons scurrying inside the air-conditioned shop. The coffee house was a well-known student hangout adjacent to Tempe's ASU campus. She didn't believe anyone would notice her, let alone recognize her. She dressed casually in chinos, a short-sleeved shirt and hiking boots. A down vest hung on the back of the chair. Dark aviator glasses cut down the glare of the early afternoon and hid her blue eyes. The brim of an Australian oil hat was pulled down low over her brow, shading her narrow face and aquiline nose. Her brown hair was cut short and dyed blond.

She glanced at her watch, a gift from her father on the day of her emancipation. The old analog time piece didn't have any smart features, but she didn't care. The sentimentality was the only thing that mattered. Quarter to one. Zack should be here any minute.

Sipping her espresso, she scanned the area around the coffee house. She saw no one suspicious. At least she wasn't being followed. That hadn't always been the case since her father was murdered nine months ago. On five different occasions, she'd had to shake tails to be safe.

She furled her lower lip in her teeth, picturing her father, willing herself to recall his exact words to her on her twelfth birthday. He had taken her outside, away from the other girls and boys invited to her party, by the willow tree in their backyard and the tire swing he had put up for her.

"You wouldn't let anyone swing on the tire," he said eyeing the chain that held the tire.

"I ... can't. I ..." She added hastily, "Take it down. It's going to break for whoever uses it next."

He studied her, head cocked to one side as if seeing something hidden deep within a prism. "You saw this happen."

She nodded.

"You see these things often?"

She nodded again. "But they don't always come true, except ... like when Nana died when I was four."

"Go on."

Sarah looked back at the house and the kids gathered there. "The party..."

"They'll wait. This is important."

She told him every freaky vision she'd had for the past eight years. Her journey into the realm of precognition began at the tender age of four with a dream that pierced the veil of time. That night, in the quiet whispers of her altered state, she foresaw the passing of her grandmother. The weight of this revelation was hers alone to bear, and she chose to keep the knowledge locked within her heart. This event was but the first of many visions, and some were frightening.

Sarah soon realized these "funny little dreams" were not the product of a child's overactive imagination. With time, she learned these glimpses into the future—though not always precise, their accuracy ebbing and flowing like the tides—were a special precognitive talent.

"And now, on your twelfth birthday, you know these aren't just dreams."

Sarah scowled. "Whatever is happening to me, it's terrible ... a curse."

Her father smiled. "Not a curse but a talent. A kind of super-human skill—a latent ability that many people possess yet few acknowledge or trust."

"It doesn't seem like that to me. I have these weird, terrible visions over and over. A fire descends from the sky and burns everything on the planet. Everything it touches."

His eyes widened. "Is it the same vision?"

She nodded. "Yes, though sometimes it starts differently. A woman screaming, like Mama when I was born."

Her father pushed away from the tree. "You remember that?" he asked earnestly.

"Sure." She picked at a hangnail. "I know this will sound silly, but it's like I'm having somebody else's vision."

He shook his head. "Do you have many of these kinds of visions?"

"No. Just a few. One was nothing but a dark empty void, but I was somehow in it. It was terrifying. I wish I could see something better."

He leaned back against the willow, a smile once more on his full lips. "Better visions will come, Sarah."

"How do you know?"

"There are people working very hard at constructing the brighter future you can be a part of."

He looked at the house, and she followed his gaze. Her mother waved at them from the sliding glass doors that led onto the patio. "It's time for you to blow out candles and cut the cake."

"Do I have to?"

"Yes. You have obligations as the birthday girl."

She made a face at him then took his hand and walked toward the house.

Sarah checked her watch again. It was five til one. She sat back against the chair and looked at the Kranzler Café's empty parking lot. She frowned. Zack was late. They could make up some time on the four-lane highway heading north to Sedona, but if they were delayed too long, the old Indian shaman wouldn't wait for them. The part of her vision that had told her to take Zack to the old shaman had not revealed anything about them being late. Other complications loomed in the edges of her vision, figures that seemed more like shadows than real people.

I wish my talent was more precise. Sarah's father had never tried to teach her how to use it. He told her he couldn't.

As Sarah navigated life, her precognitive abilities intertwined with her existence, their clarity sharpened in moments of personal crisis or when others were in peril. Her prescient ability lent her a sense of omnipotence, compelling her to intervene when foresight and reality collided. Despite her efforts, she estimated her predictions bore fruit only twenty percent of the time. Yet the dark, dystopian dreams persisted, unyielding and unending.

A turning point came when Sarah stumbled upon a book titled *Imagination* by an author she revered as a creator of worlds. The premise was simple yet profound: without the capacity to imagine, creation is impossible. This principle, suggesting the dawn of a new physics probing the essence of life itself, resonated deeply with Sarah. It inspired her to envision the utopia her father hinted at a decade earlier. A harmonious existence for humanity and the planet. Despite her fervent attempts to see this vision become a reality, success remained elusive, a dream beyond the horizon.

The narrative took a surreal turn when Sarah's visions repeatedly showcased a man, a harbinger of ominous outcomes. He seemed desperate to convey a message, one intrinsically linked to the power of imagination. *I have yet to meet him, but I will meet him.*

A western banded gecko climbed the wall of the coffee house. It moved with the skill of an accomplished gymnast. Her foot ached where she had broken it more than year ago. It seemed always to hurt when something life-altering approached.

Car tires crunched gravel in the café's parking lot. Two men got out of the back seat of an Uber. She recognized the tall, rangy features of Zack Helm instantly. The other man's back was to her as he pulled a daypack from the back seat. He turned, and her stomach twisted. The man from her premonitions. Not quite as tall as Zack, thinner, with graying hair and ruddy cheeks.

In the space of a heartbeat, Sarah understood their destinies were intertwined, a revelation that promised to unlock the secrets of imagination and pave the way for the future she had longed to manifest in a way she never understood, in a way that was greater than herself alone.

6

———

THE SHAMAN
SEDONA, ARIZONA

The old Indian shaman sat under the shade of the bus stop canopy erected at the turnoff from Highway 89A heading east. Slender ash poles cast a slatted shadow over him. Smoke from his cigarette rose lazily in the cool air. He lifted the gray battered Stetson and used it to shade his eyes against the sun, already descending westward into the crisp fall afternoon. He measured the distance above the western horizon and felt the approaching presence of another man he knew well.

He wondered again how the young woman found him or how she knew about the cave. Only a few were aware of its existence. He would have hung up on her except she told him the numbers.

"1162413," she said.

"Hmmm," he answered. "What do they mean to you?"

"I haven't figured that out yet," she admitted.

He paused for three heartbeats. "Who sent you?"

"My father—Simon Ravensbach—and General Deke Davidson."

"Be at the turnoff at mile marker 365 on Highway 89A on September twenty-ninth, no later than three in the afternoon." He hung up.

The shaman cleared his mind, going through the ritual of letting the physical world be there and not be there, everything around him a mere product of his senses. His thoughts emptied, and he waited.

* * *

Sarah Davenport navigated the Tesla through the chaotic weave of I-17 traffic, her movements sharp and fluid, like the skilled athlete she was. She barely noticed the towering Saguaros flashing by, too focused on the looming appointment in Sedona. They were late, and missing this meeting with the shaman was not an option.

With a quick, deliberate motion, Sarah activated the Tesla's autopilot, relinquishing the wheel to the machine. She turned toward the back seat where Johns, pale and uneasy, sat stiffly. His eyes flicked nervously between the road ahead and the now-unattended steering wheel.

"You look like you've got questions," Sarah said, her voice tinged with something between amusement and challenge.

Johns hesitated then blurted out, "What does this place we're going to have to do with the Eleusinian mysteries?"

She smiled faintly, her gaze shifting as if considering how much to reveal. "A friend of my father's connected me with someone—a shaman. Says the site we're heading to holds something linked to Eleusis, the ancient city near Athens."

Johns' brow furrowed; his interest piqued despite himself. "Your father?"

"Simon Ravensbach," she said evenly, the name carrying weight. "He passed away not long ago."

"I'm sorry," Johns said softly, his voice betraying a familiar ache. "I lost my wife not too long ago, too."

Sarah's eyes flickered for a moment, a shadow of shared pain crossing her face. "The world's a mess," she muttered.

Zack, silent until now, shifted in the front seat, his voice low and casual. "It sure can be."

Sarah glanced at Johns, noting the lingering grief in his expression. She softened, if only slightly. "So, why'd you agree to come along?"

Johns hesitated, staring out the window as if searching for an answer in the passing desert. "I last visited Eleusis a few years ago," he finally said, his voice distant. "But why would a Native American shaman care about an ancient Greek city?"

A laugh bubbled up from Sarah, sharp and unexpected. "The guy who hooked me up said this shaman was there when Socrates had his big awakening at Eleusis."

Johns blinked, caught off guard. "You can't be serious."

"The shaman was," Sarah replied with a smirk.

"You're talking about the Hindu concept of reincarnation, where the being or soul moves from one bodily incarnation to another?" Johns asked, his tone skeptical.

Sarah shrugged, eyes glinting. "Maybe."

Johns' unease deepened. He turned to Zack, his voice low. "This doesn't feel right. We should turn around. Head back to Phoenix."

Zack grinned, a mischievous edge to his expression. "Hold on, Isaac. There's another angle. Ever hear of remote viewing?"

Johns' eyes widened. "You mean like that military project—the Men Who Stare at Goats?"

"Exactly," Zack said, leaning back in his seat, clearly enjoying himself.

Sarah frowned, her tone more serious. "Remote viewing the past is a real thing. Some people can do it—especially shamans. Doesn't have to be reincarnation."

Johns' skepticism remained, but something in Sarah's conviction reassured him. "What else can this shaman do?"

Sarah's smile turned cryptic. "Why don't you ask him when we get there?"

Johns fell silent, leaning back and closing his eyes. Within moments, the soft sound of snoring filled the car.

"Is he really asleep?" Sarah asked, glancing at Zack.

"Yep. Fastest sleeper I know." Zack chuckled. "He's good like that."

"Where'd you find him?"

Zack's grin faded slightly. "The producer funding this whole thing said we'd lose the money if Johns didn't come along."

"Perfect," she muttered, checking her watch. Prescott was just behind them, the clock ticking past two-thirty. "We'll make it," she whispered, more to herself than anyone else.

7

THE HELICOPTER

SEDONA

The helicopter soared, and with it, Janus Snyder's heart lifted, mingling with the boundless sky. For a moment, his mind pushed him back in time to the second Iraq War. A pilot prodigy, Snyder mastered flying with the Netherlands Armed Forces in the Middle East, where the roar of helicopter blades became synonymous with fleeting freedom. The intoxicating blend of liberty and power haunted him long after his service ended.

Now, hovering over the vast expanse of northern Arizona, Snyder found his solace once more. He sensed a freedom greater than the earth and sky and ocean, his soul merging with the infinite as the Gnostics proclaimed.

Abruptly, the serenity was shattered by the intrusion of technology—a red blinking light on the tracking map. Glancing at the screen, he noted Sarah's Tesla, a vehicle he covertly tagged the previous night, was now making a beeline for Sedona.

Looking down from his aerial vantage, Snyder's vision of the world was one not of people, but of relentless technological proliferation. Cars, trucks, and innumerable cell phones sprawled across the landscape, a testament to humanity's voracious appetite for advancement. This realization stirred a tumultuous anger within him, a profound irritation at the unchecked growth of technology, outpacing human population and dwarfing the essence of the human spirit.

The thought of billions of cell phones, interlinked in a vast, soulless network, was a bitter pill to swallow. It was the crazed legacy of individuals like his parents and Sarah's father. Pioneers who pushed the boundaries of what was technologically possible, yet inadvertently steered humanity away from the path of divine love.

This was the battle Snyder found himself engaged in—a fight not just against the tide of technological dominance but against the erosion of something far more precious. The prospect of a world devoid of divine love. A world where human connections were supplanted by cold, digital interactions. The digital technological web was an affront, a sin of unimaginable magnitude. This realization fueled his resolve. Halting man's relentless march toward a disconnected future was not just a mission; it was a moral imperative. A world stripped of divine love, he mused bitterly, would be humanity's greatest downfall.

8

THE MEETING

FOREST SERVICE ROAD 525

Under a sky vast and unyielding, Sarah veered off the main highway onto Red Canyon Road, a gravel Forest Service access road. A few miles into this secluded area, she eased the Tesla into a makeshift parking lot for a trailhead. She flicked her gaze to her watch. "We're here," she announced, relieved they had reached the rendezvous point with minutes to spare.

"Where's our guide?" Johns asked.

Sarah pointed at the other vehicle in the lot, a 1992 silver Toyota Pickup 4-wheel drive with a raised camper shell.

"You sure?" Johns asked, scanning the seemingly empty surroundings. "Doesn't seem like anyone's around."

The trio stepped out of the car, the air growing heavier, almost palpable. Zack wasted no time heading straight for the trunk, his mind focused on the equipment inside. For him, this moment wasn't just about the strange journey they were on—it marked the start of what he hoped would be a pivotal career move.

Sarah, on the other hand, lingered near the car, her eyes following Zack and Isaac. She hesitated, wondering if she should share her plans before the shaman arrived. But something made her hold back. She decided to wait.

Johns, feeling out of place in the unfamiliar high desert, wandered a short distance away from the group. The stark landscape unsettled him—the blazing sun above contrasting with the cool, crisp air at this high altitude. The emptiness gnawed at him, and the absence of their shaman guide only heightened his discomfort. What were they doing out here, so far from anything familiar?

Peering into the truck's cab, Johns' eyes caught on an AR-15. His stomach lurched. *Christ*, he thought, panic rising. *What have I gotten myself into?* He took a deep breath, ready to call out to the others about his disturbing find, when something even more unsettling happened.

A strange sensation washed over him, like the world had subtly shifted, revealing a layer of reality he hadn't known existed. His breath caught in his throat as he turned, expecting to see nothing— yet standing there, impossibly, was Professor R. S. Seaford, his PhD advisor. The man had died five years ago.

Johns blinked, his heart racing, and the image wavered. The figure morphed into someone else—a short, slightly chubby man wearing regular clothes, a dusty black hat with an eagle feather tucked into the band, and a medicine pouch adorned with intricate beadwork depicting a wolf hanging around his neck. The transformation felt as surreal as it was unsettling.

The man's gaze fixed on Johns, sharp and knowing, like he could see straight through him.

"Who... who are you?" Johns stammered, his voice barely audible.

"I'm your guide," the figure responded, his tone directed at Johns with unnerving certainty.

Johns signaled to Zack and Sarah indicating the guide was here.

Zack, ever the documentarian, grabbed his camera and began filming. The shaman admonished him to put the camera away. Zack nodded and set the camera on the hood of the car pointed at the shaman.

A muffled exchange between Sarah and the guide left Johns with new questions. Through it all Zack remained unconcerned, whistling as if he hadn't a care in the world.

"Christ, Zack, doesn't any of this bother you?" Johns whispered, glancing at the mysterious guide.

Zack grinned. "Isaac, old buddy, I've been in stranger situations than this. Besides, I've got it handled." He glanced at the camera.

The lens cap was off and the red record light on. The camera bore silent witness to what was happening before their eyes.

The conversation ended and everyone moved at once except for Johns. The shaman went to his truck. Zack retrieved his camera. Sarah came over to Johns. He asked her if she was sure this was the right guy, since he didn't look like a typical Indian shaman.

Sarah blinked in surprise. "He's a respected elder among the Zunis. You can tell by the regalia he's wearing—the eagle headdress, colorful clothes, and the beaded medicine pouch at his waist."

Johns shook his head. *Who's she kidding? The guy looks like a bum from Skid Row.*

"There's been a change of plans," Sarah said, her tone calm but with an edge that hinted at something unsaid. "You and Zack won't need blindfolds after all. You'll ride in the back of his truck."

Johns' eyes darted to the blacked-out windows of the truck's topper, a prickle of unease creeping up his spine. He watched as the shaman silently helped Zack load the film equipment into the front seat, his movements deliberate and steady. Johns couldn't shake the feeling there was more going on here than Sarah was letting on.

"Any more surprises?" Johns asked, his voice edged with tension.

Sarah glanced at him, her expression unreadable. "I'm not coming with you," she said finally. "The shaman says there's another path for me, and it's not what's about to unfold for you at the cave."

Johns blinked in surprise. He wasn't exactly thrilled about venturing into the remote wilderness of Coconino National Forest without Sarah—the person who had set up this trek. And now he was heading into the unknown, guided by a cryptic shaman and armed only with Zack's film equipment.

Zack, however, didn't seem fazed. He grabbed the camera, grinning as he clambered into the truck bed like a man setting off on an adventure. Reluctantly, Johns followed him, glancing once more at

Sarah. His last glimpse of her was through the dusty haze as she got into her Tesla and drove off, leaving the parking area behind. The blacked-out door to the topper was closed behind them and locked.

The truck's engine growled to life, and without warning, it lurched forward, gravel crunching beneath the tires as they sped down the desolate road. The blacked-out windows swallowed any view of the outside world, leaving Johns in darkness as they plunged deeper into the heart of the forest.

9

EXECUTIVE PRODUCER

SANTA MONICA PIER, CALIFORNIA

ONE MONTH AGO

The Santa Monica Pier jutted out into the Pacific Ocean at the intersection of Colorado and Ocean. The glamorous structure was one of the most iconic locations in the world.

At the pier's edge, Zack Helm leaned against the railing, immersed in the spectacle of the setting sun melting into the ocean. Behind him, the Ferris Wheel's neon lights blazed into life against a dusky sky, while beachgoers began their evening exodus, their laughter and chatter a backdrop to the transitioning day.

The pier, quieting down, felt like an odd choice for a meeting. It reminded Zack of a scene from *NCIS: Los Angeles*, stirring a mix of anticipation and apprehension within him.

His phone buzzed. "Zack Helms," he answered, speaker on.

A man chuckled. "Look to your left."

Turning, Zack spotted an older man in a linen suit and bow tie, his look completed with a walking cane and battered fedora. Sam Hill, one of Hollywood's elite executive producers, was unmistakable.

He strolled over to Zack. "You know who I am?" Sam's handshake was firm, his grin genuine—a rarity in their industry.

"Who in this town doesn't?" Zack retorted, earning a laugh from Sam. "My agent was vague about the details. Why here?"

"Your documentaries are quite the moneymakers." Sam glanced around the now quiet pier. "Let's cut to the chase."

Zack's heart raced. A collaboration with Sam Hill could be the breakthrough he needed. "I'm listening."

"That documentary series you did five years ago—*In Search of Lost Places* ... I particularly liked the program when you were looking for the lost city of gold."

"*Coronado and the Seven Cities of Cibola.* My favorite too."

"That's the one. I have an idea for a series like it."

Zack leaned against the iron railing and forced his heart to beat slowly. If he hooked up with Sam Hill, his money troubles would be over. "Okay, I'm getting excited."

Sam outlined his vision for the *cinema vérité*-driven series, a blend of adventure and mystery, centered around the possibility of ancient ruins in the new world. The concept was ambitious, the kind that could captivate audiences worldwide. "What I need from you is a sizzle reel."

Zack nodded. A sizzle reel was the cinematic version of the infamous Hollywood elevator pitch. "What's it pay?"

"Fifty grand, just for the reel. Plus, if you impress the networks, you're on board as the producer. Can you deliver?" Sam's eyes twinkled with challenge.

The offer was staggering. Zack pushed himself upright and stuck out his hand. "I'm your man." They shook. "What are these ruins?"

"An alleged ancient Greek structure in the northern Arizona desert."

"Greek?"

"Uh-huh. Legends say this lost place is connected to the mystery schools north of Athens."

Zack's brain was already buzzing. *Greek mystery schools ... Eleusinian ... shit. This is the dream I've wanted since Princeton.* He managed to keep his voice matter of fact. "I like it."

"Good. I want you to follow the same format as *In Search of Lost Places,* including the interaction between the local and an expert who've never met before."

"Yeah, that was a sweet dynamic. Who's the local?"

"A woman named Sarah Davenport. She knows everyone in northern Arizona. You'll be operating out of Sedona, by the way."

Zack laughed. "Vortex capital of the world."

Sam Hill grinned. "Thought that might grab you."

"Who's the expert?"

"Professor Isaac Johns." He paused, searching Zack's face. "You went to school with him, right?"

"Princeton. We were roommates."

"We need him on this."

"What if I can't get him?"

"Then the deal's off."

Zack clenched his teeth at the finality in Hill's tone. *He really wants Isaac. I'm just the middleman.* "I'll get him."

"Good. Don't let anybody know about this; we can't have some other studio jumping on the premise before we get this done. You know Hollywood."

"Of course."

They shook hands again.

"I'll have my team put the deal together with your agent. Johns is at ASU in Tempe on sabbatical."

As they parted ways, the pier, now lively with night visitors, echoed Zack's surge of enthusiasm. Despite the lingering questions and the shadows of doubt, the opportunity was too thrilling to pass up. Crossing to his favorite bar, Zack couldn't help but feel the night was a harbinger of exciting times ahead. Santa Monica Pier had set the stage, and he was ready to dive into the adventure.

10

THE RIDE

COCONINO NATIONAL FOREST, ARIZONA

Using the soft glow of his cell phone, Zack managed to pry the blackened window open a few inches, inviting a stream of fresh air into the cramped topper. The light cast faint shadows against the dark interior, evoking a philosophical reflection from Johns. "Feels like Plato's cave."

"Reminds me more of *The Matrix*," Zack added, drawing a parallel to their surreal predicament.

Inside the topper, the heat was oppressive. A sheet of thin foam on the steel bed did little to soften the relentless jolts from potholes dotting the Forest Service road. Both men pulled out bottled water from their backpacks.

"Sorry about this. It's not what I expected," Zack lamented.

Johns, curiosity piqued, stretched out his legs. "Honestly, Zack, how did we end up in the back of a truck, windows blackened, heading to God only knows where?"

As Zack recounted the curious chain of events starting from a meeting on the Santa Monica Pier, Johns listened intently, his tongue clicking against the roof of his mouth—a nervous habit Zack remembered from their student days at Princeton.

"So why did you pick me as the expert on Eleusis? It's hardly my specialty, and others are much more qualified."

Zack offered a smile, unwilling to tell the truth. "We always dreamed about doing an adventure together back in the day. Seemed like a good time to do it."

The truck lurched violently, and the two men were thrown against the sides. Johns righted himself. "Maybe, that is. Why'd you wait until the last minute to ask me?"

"I figured if you had enough time to think about it, you wouldn't do it. I needed the urgency to do it right now, today."

"So ... you manipulated me."

"It's necessary in my business. Besides, it worked, didn't it?"

The truck rocked again, and Johns spilled water down his pants. Zack grinned.

Johns snorted. "What do you know about Sarah?"

"Apart from the obvious—young, beautiful, and smart—I was told she's been investigating multiple paranormal phenomena in the area, including Bradshaw ranch. We've spoken on the phone a few times."

The truck slowed, and both men braced themselves for another lurch. They rolled quietly through a dip before the truck picked up speed again.

"Our shaman seems to be in a hurry," Johns said.

"The sun will set around six tonight. He probably wants to get us to the cave and back again before dark."

"So, leaving Sarah behind was unexpected?"

"Absolutely."

Johns threshed his hair. "Do you get a sense this was all orchestrated?"

A long pause stretched as Zack leaned against the window and sucked in fresh air. He folded his legs and said, "I can see that."

"The shaman has a rifle."

"I saw it."

Johns looked at his water bottle and decided against it. They were rolling along pretty fast, but there was no telling when they'd hit another pothole. "There's something strange about him. First, for a moment I thought I saw one of my professors then the shaman suddenly appeared."

"Suddenly?"

"Like he was beamed down or something. I saw a balding older gentleman, nothing like what I expected for a shaman. Yet he was strangely familiar. When I described to Sarah what he looked like, she saw something quite different."

"What did she see?"

"A man dressed in typical Southwest Native American regalia."

"Interesting. You know, I've done several docs on reservations. There's always a couple of men who look like the classic strong Indian warrior. For me, the shaman fits that bill."

Johns creased his forehead and started clicking his tongue again. Finally, he pointed to Zack's camera. "You filmed some of the interactions between the shaman and Sarah. Can we take a look at what you filmed?"

Zack nodded. "Bring your phone's flashlight over here." He adjusted the camera for playback and pressed play. Sarah was speaking with the shaman, but the man wasn't there.

"Shit," Zack muttered.

Johns pointed to a small white dot moving around in the frame. "What's that? Back scatter? Lens defect?"

"No." Zack studied the image and the white dot moving erratically. "Damn, I wouldn't have believed it possible."

"What are you talking about, man?"

"On the reservations, there's always talk about shape shifters. The Navajo call them Skinwalkers. It's also said many shamans themselves are shape shifters–that they can move between realities. They're guardians of sacred places."

"You believe that?"

"Maybe I do now."

The ride became violent, bouncing and swaying with great intensity.

Zack said, "We're definitely off-road now."

"Ya think?"

The two men braced themselves, laughing hysterically at the absurdity of the situation they found themselves in.

Once the truck settled down, Zack asked, "Isaac, you afraid to die?"

"You first."

"I'm terrified. Now you."

"After my wife died, I became obsessed with death. I looked into near-death experiences. Even went to a major conference and talked to many experiencers on the numerous panels. What they said varied greatly, but many claimed they lost all fear of death."

"I suppose if you experience it once, a second time doesn't have the same visceral reaction."

Johns nodded. "I even took hallucinogens."

"Seriously? That doesn't sound like you."

"I know, I've got to believe in providence. By the way, most scholars believe the Greek initiates who went to Eleusis to wake up to the greater truth took hallucinogens. Although, nobody's been able to identify the chemical they might've used."

The two men lurched forward as the truck halted. They waited until the shaman came around and opened the back of the topper.

"Get your film gear. We need to get moving." The shaman left the two men to stretch and get their bearings.

Johns whispered to Zack, "How did he look to you?"

"The same as before."

"That's what I see now, thank God."

The shaman reappeared, carrying the black rifle loosely. "We have to go now." He set off between two large ponderosa pines.

Zack and Johns scrambled after him.

11

A SHOCK

COCONINO NATIONAL FOREST, ARIZONA

Janus Snyder checked the Arctic P9 Military telescope mounted on the Bell helicopter's flight deck. The scope, created at Johns Hopkins University using nano-array and thin film mosaic technology, was a marvel. It was capable of a maximum magnification 300 times that of ordinary telescopes of the same diameter. The most compelling feature, however, was the telescope's Bluetooth technology integrated with the helicopter's on board systems, casting real-time images directly onto the flight deck's monitor. From his aerial vantage, Snyder tracked Sarah's Tesla with ease, a silent shadow five miles distant. He felt a surge of anticipation when she veered off the main road south of Sedona and parked at a Forest Service trailhead.

He observed Sarah, alongside the documentary filmmaker and the ancient Greek historian, approach an old Toyota truck with a blacked-out camper top. Nonplussed that the trio's guide seemed to be nowhere around, Snyder adjusted the telescope's aperture to take in a wider view. A shimmer of light and an old man abruptly appeared.

Troubled by the sudden materialization, Snyder stared at the image on the screen for a moment. His hands tightened on the controls, and he forced himself to breathe slowly. His contact had told him the escort was not a local tour guide making a few bucks but a Native American shaman with unusual capabilities. The revelation did nothing to shake Snyder's resolve. If anything, it steeled his determination.

Snyder watched the old Toyota truck dart down the forest road, vanishing into the embrace of the densely wooded hills, while Sarah Davenport drove off in her Tesla back toward Sedona.

The mission had been clear: track Sarah and her companions to the cave then erase it from existence. The essence of his task had been crystallized during the pivotal phone call with his contact. The question of why the cave must be destroyed opened for Snyder a window into a realm of intrigue and hidden agendas. His contact's revelation that a ritual performed in the cave had inadvertently birthed a new paradigm of human potential only deepened the mystery. The man told him, "I was one of the first to participate in a ritual at a different cave site founded earlier with Simon Ravensbach and others, like your parents. Though we didn't know it at the time, we ... all of us were part of an extraordinary transformation capable of bringing about a new type of human. In fact, that is the singularity we must stop."

Snyder's directive was uncomplicated—obliterate the cave and deal with the aftermath as he saw fit, with one non-negotiable condition: Sarah Davenport must remain unharmed.

The caveat surprised Snyder. After all, he killed Sarah's father. "Why is she so important?"

"Before Simon Ravensbach died, he gave his daughter a set of numbers. No one knows what these numbers mean, but they must be important. You are to follow her and see what these numbers mean."

"Copy that." Snyder felt unaccountably nervous, a feeling he hadn't experienced since his two tours in Iraq. Brushing aside the feeling, he asked point blank, "Who are you? Why are you going to such great lengths to stop these people?"

The contact chuckled at the other end. "Our strength is in our anonymity." The connection went dead.

His conversation with the anonymous strategist left Snyder with doubts, but at the time he resolved to follow the plan, as it served his own interests.

Snyder caught glimpses of the truck as it slipped away through the trees. Sarah sped toward Sedona. The numbers she carried were important, but so was the location of the cave. Snyder glanced at the explosives lying next to his dog. He ran through the possibilities and decided the best interests of the plan were achieved by tailing Sarah.

He turned the helicopter to follow her. Abruptly, Snyder felt the presence of his contact, as if the man were somehow observing him. His nostrils flared and his lips thinned at the pervasive sense of being watched by his unseen contact. *Christos! He's a fucking remote viewer.* Gritting his teeth against the intrusion, Snyder backed away from his choice and set off in pursuit of the truck. Sarah's information, for now, would be out of reach.

12

WHO IS THE SHAMAN?

COCONINO FOREST

Johns labored to keep pace with the shaman. The air was sultry, and within minutes he was drenched with sweat. The old man moved with remarkable ease through the rough terrain, shouldering Zack's heavy film equipment pack without effort.

The trail dissolved into a dense thicket of pinion pine and junipers. The shaman, undeterred by the maze of intertwining branches, pressed forward as if guided by an unseen force. Cursing, Johns followed, shielding his face from the thorny limbs. Behind him, Zack laughed and said, "Relax, Isaac. This is like when we were young, playing Indiana Jones."

The other side opened onto a narrow creek filled with rushing water that whispered ancient untold secrets. The shaman beckoned them forward, hopping from one bank to the other with a nimbleness that defied his age. Johns followed, hiking shoes betraying him on the slick stones lining the creek. More than once, he found himself kept upright by the shaman's gentle grip.

Zack, ever the documentarian, called for intermittent halts, dashing ahead to capture on film their journey through the untamed wilderness.

The path led them along a game trail that wound through a

vast, towering cathedral of ancient spruce and fir trees. The immense forest giants stretched high above, casting a dim, twilight gloom over the earth below. Johns tilted his head slightly, listening intently to the profound silence that surrounded them. The forest was eerily still, as if holding its breath. The shaman moved like a phantom, leaving no sound, no trace, while Johns' and Zack's footprints were the only evidence anyone had passed through. To Johns, it felt as if they had stepped into a realm of magic—an ancient world, untouched and sacred, as though time itself had stopped in deference to the forest's age-old secrets.

They kept a brisk pace until they came upon a colossal fallen tree, its massive roots splayed out like the remnants of an old, forgotten sentinel.

As they paused, Zack, breathing heavily, saw his chance. "I want you guys to sit for a moment and have a conversation I can film," he said, using the moment to catch his breath.

The old Indian, amused but compliant, stopped. Johns was happy to rest. His feet ached from trekking through the pathless forest. He was hungry and out of breath. The pair settled onto the log, Johns letting his day pack slide carelessly to the ground. He reached for a water bottle, but the shaman stopped him with a shake of his head. Despite his thirst, Johns obeyed.

Without waiting for Zack's signal, Johns asked, "What do I call you?"

The shaman gazed at a sliver of sky cradled by the forest's lush canopy for a long time before answering. "The Hopi elders have given me many names. Today, I am Crowfoot."

"You've had other names?"

The old man merely nodded, prompting Johns to shift the conversation.

"Sarah told me you were present when Socrates did his initiation at Eleusis."

The shaman's gaze sharpened, piercing Johns with an intensity that forced him to avert his eyes. When he dared look again, the shaman spoke, his voice carrying the weight of eons. "I see your soul, Dr. Isaac Johns."

"I feel it." Johns admitted, a sense of awe enveloping him.

"There is more you should know. I am ancient ... I have always been ... I was there when the first human awoke from the darkness ... when Socrates awoke ... when Jesus awoke ... when Rumi awoke ... I was there when Mirabai found the light. She was special." He paused, letting his words sink in. He continued, his voice a whisper. "I witnessed Steve Jobs envision the future of communication. I am a part of all, waiting to be acknowledged, to be embraced."

Johns slipped into an altered state of consciousness. A beam of pure love enveloped him. It penetrated his entire being, an over-whelming realization that affirmed the shaman's timeless presence across epochs. "There's more, isn't there?"

The shaman continued, the words entering John's mind telepathically, in a type of communication Johns had heard called mindspeak. It was more than words; it was feelings and thoughts that came from the core of their beings. "The mysteries deepen, spiraling into realms where total knowledge resides. This is the essence of Eleusis, the truth awaiting initiates within the cave."

As reality reasserted itself, Johns' anticipation for the cave and its hidden truths surged. "How much longer till we reach the cave?"

The shaman locked eyes again with him, an intense gaze that pierced his very soul. "We are close, Isaac Johns."

Johns flinched under the stare, but he was determined. "I'm okay. I'm ready to go," he insisted, his thirst and hunger somehow abated by the shaman's gaze.

"I sense you are troubled by your wife's death, wondering about the afterlife and if you might reunite with her again."

"That's the real reason I'm here right now, the possibility of near-death experiences."

Zack, unaware of the depth of their connection, interrupted, "That was great."

The shaman stood abruptly, his expression darkening as his voice took on a grave urgency. "We must move quickly. We are not alone," he warned, his eyes scanning the treetops. "A helicopter has been tracking us."

Before Johns or Zack could fully grasp his words, the unmistakable *thwop, thwop, thwop* of helicopter rotors sliced through the silence, growing louder with every second. The city dwellers froze, their hearts pounding as the sound echoed above them. They craned their necks upward, and there it was—the helicopter, a menacing silhouette against the sky, circling like a predator.

The sight jolted them, a stark and terrifying reminder of the modern world intruding upon this ancient, sacred place. Zack's voice cracked the tension, his breathless "Christ!" reverberating through the stillness of the forest, a cry swallowed by the looming trees and impending danger.

13

THE CHASE
COCONINO FOREST

From his vantage point a thousand feet in the air, Snyder's gaze followed the three men as they vanished into the dense fir and spruce forest, the canopy so thick he quickly lost sight of them. He grimaced that his chance of destroying the cave might be slipping away.

Snyder glanced nervously at the fuel gauge, his jaw tightening as he saw they had only a couple of hours left. His pulse quickened. Time was running out. The rhythmic thrum of the helicopter blades, usually a steadying presence, became a countdown, each beat tightening the knot of anxiety in his chest.

"We'll have to land and track them on foot, boy."

Hearing his master's voice, Turk sat up and peered through the helicopter's plastex canopy as if he could spot their quarry. He growled, eager to begin the chase.

Snyder expertly maneuvered the helicopter to land in a parking area, narrowly avoiding the shaman's Toyota with its darkened topper by mere inches. He cursed under his breath at the urgency of their situation. The possibility of someone investigating what they might assume to be a downed helicopter pressed on him.

Turk bounded out the door as the helicopter blades stilled. Snyder followed, grabbing his backpack filled with explosives and slinging the sniper rifle over his shoulder. Though eager to track the men, he first searched the Toyota for anything Turk could use to track their prey.

Frustration boiled over as he realized they had taken every scrap of clothing with them. He pounded a fist on the hood. *That old Indian's clever ... but not that clever.* "Hiel, Turk," he called, using the Dutch commands he'd been trained with. The dog ran to his side, and they scoured the clearing. Snyder stopped beside a scrub oak where the ground was wet. The scent of urine might lead them to their quarry.

"Finden," he commanded, and they set off at a jog, Turk leading with his nose in the air, pulled forward by the scent of the man who took a leak.

As they navigated the rugged terrain, Snyder's thoughts drifted to his parents, who according to his contact had entered a similar cave. Had they ventured together or alone? Did they enter the cave before or after his birth? He pondered how different his life might have been if they had chosen a different path.

Turk's worried whine snapped Snyder back to the present. The shepherd paced anxiously in front of a stand of pines. He'd lost the scent. Snyder knelt and discovered the telltale brush marks left by a pine bough.

"Damn!" Snyder exploded, frustration and fear of failure crashing down on him. He realized the depth of his adversary's cunning too late. Placing his backpack down, he laid his sniper rifle atop it, the weight of his mission's potential failure bearing down on him with overwhelming force.

Scratching at the scar on his forehead, Snyder closed his eyes and let go of all thoughts, allowing the way in front of him to open. Within moments, a bolt of heightened awareness surged through his body, igniting a psychic ability that usually lay dormant until needed. Suddenly, with clarity that transcended the ordinary, he saw in his mind's eye the precise location of the shaman. This vision showed Snyder exactly where he needed to go.

This extraordinary gift first revealed itself in the harsh landscapes of Iraq. Snyder was recognized to possess what military circles reverently termed the "point man syndrome"—a phenomenon documented since the Vietnam War, where certain individuals had the uncanny ability to sense or see danger before it manifested. Those with this gift, when leading a patrol, ensured the safety of everyone. Their insights allowed them to challenge orders from higher-ups based on their supernatural intuitions. Sometimes, this ability manifested as a gut feeling; other times, it was visual—a mental image of enemies lying in ambush, or even phantoms foretelling peril.

Snyder vividly recalled the awakening of his abilities. In Basra, during patrols, his psychic insights saved his squad more times than he could count. All except for the last day, when a newly appointed British lieutenant, part of a NATO exchange program, dismissed Snyder's warnings.

"Our objective is at the end of this street," the lieutenant declared as they huddled behind a sunbaked mudbrick building in the old part of the city. "The way's clear. We go in, get the informant, and we're out again." He ordered the men forward, but Snyder stood his ground. "Janus, that's an order. Get moving."

"No, sir. If you lead us down this street, you'll get us all killed."

"What the hell are you talking about?"

Snyder conveyed the danger he had foreseen. "It's a trap, sir. The informant is dead."

"You can't know that. Move!"

But Snyder refused, and the tension among the squad members rose palpably. An older sergeant, who trusted Snyder's intuition, supported him, "Sir, if Janus says we'll get killed walking down that street, then we're walking into a death trap."

The lieutenant, stubborn to the core, insisted, "We're going down that street. That's an order."

He had barely taken a dozen steps into the alley when a sniper's bullet ended his life. Two more men were seriously wounded in the effort to retrieve his body and a ricochet creased Snyder's scalp.

Now, threading through the maze of pinyon pines and junipers with Turk by his side, that same inexplicable force guided him. "This way, Turk," he murmured, trusting the psychic pull through the dense thicket of trees and underbrush toward their quarry.

14

THE SEDONA CAVE
COCONINO FOREST

The shaman spurred Johns and Zack out of the small clearing with an urgency that bordered on desperation. He went off the trail, navigating a steep slope strewn with loose stones. At the bottom, jagged boulders awaited the three men. A single misstep could end in disaster.

Miraculously, they reached the other side unscathed. Their guide pushed them to quicken their pace even more for an hour and a half. They didn't halt their breakneck pace until they came to a towering cliff.

The old Indian scanned the area. "We are safe for now," he assured them, before edging along a narrow trail that hugged the cliff base, vanishing after a dozen steps.

Johns set down his pack and studied the sheer rock face, a breathtaking canvas of indigenous petroglyphs meticulously etched into the desert varnish coating of the Jurassic Age rock panels. The symbols held him in awe.

While Johns stood engrossed, Zack captured both wide and tight angle shots of the ancient imagery. "Great stuff, huh, Isaac?"

"Yeah ... great stuff. Make sure you get a good shot of that spiral. It's the universal symbol of a portal to another world."

"Who did this?"

Johns said the art was attributed to a Puebloan culture. "The Sinagua. They were contemporaries of the Anasazi and occupied the area around Sedona from approximately 500 CE to 1425 CE. This is clearly a sacred site for them."

"But?" Zack prompted.

"Some of the symbols shouldn't be here. Like the one at the top. It looks like a UFO."

"So? Native Americans had aliens in their mythology. Many indigenous cultures believe in star people coming from a nonphysical realm."

Zack aimed his camera at a humanoid figure with large eyes and shot the image. "What do you make of that?" he asked, his tone a mixture of sarcasm and intrigue.

Johns' answer was cut off by the shaman's sudden return. "We need to go." Beckoning the two men to hurry, he led them across the cliff base through a narrow passageway among gigantic boulders to a vast opening leading to an amazing cave. The shaman said, "The Sinagua did their ceremonies in there." Inside, a single shaft of light from above eerily illuminated an immense cavern.

Zack unpacked portable LED lights. As they powered up one by one, the cave walls showed a maze of symbols Johns recognized as a mixture of ancient Greek and Sinagua. Others were mathematical formulas.

But even more incongruous was a hospital bed surrounded by a ventilator and monitors for brain and heart activity. In one corner stood a portable generator and several small tanks of propane. The hospital equipment, thick with cobwebs, looked outdated, perhaps twenty years old.

As Zack started filming, he muttered, "Judging by the age of these machines and the state of everything, I'd say they left this place in a rush about three years ago."

Johns turned to the shaman. "What the hell was going on here?"

The old Indian didn't answer but walked over to a recessed corner. Pulling back rocks, he reached into a darkened alcove and retrieved a foot-long, heavy object wrapped in deer hide. He handed it to Johns. "Open it," he commanded.

Aware Zack was filming everything, Johns carefully removed the deer hide cover. "My God!" he gasped, gaping at the treasure he held —a limestone Euphrates votive relief tablet from Eleusis, known to every Greek scholar as "the Eye." His mind raced. He had seen the Eye once before at the National Archaeological Museum in Athens. *This has got to be a replica. Or is the one in the museum a fake?*

At the top was the image of Athena, the Greek Goddess of wisdom, with rays of the sun radiating downward. The light symbolized enlightenment, knowledge, and understanding. In the religious context of the Eleusinian Mysteries, such imagery represented the illumination or spiritual insight from participation in the mysteries, or the divine revelation bestowed upon the initiate who traveled to Eleusis. *Christ! Are the Eleusinian rituals somehow playing out here?*

He pulled his gaze away from the stone tablet to the shaman. "Who gave this to you?"

"No time for explanations. Take it with you. Leave the equipment. We need to go now."

Johns re-wrapped the tablet and tucked it into his backpack while Zack gathered his lights. The three men filed out of the cave, Johns in the lead.

As soon as Johns emerged from the narrow passageway, his heart lurched. He caught a fleeting glimpse of a man, rifle raised, aiming straight at them. Before he could react, the shaman yanked him aside with lightning speed, and then fired a shot. The gunman ducked behind a tree, narrowly avoiding the bullet.

"Shit, we're trapped!" Zack gasped, clutching the camera to his chest, his voice edged with panic.

"Not yet," the shaman responded coolly, his voice laced with a strange calm, as if he welcomed the danger. His eyes gleamed with determination, unfazed by the threat ahead. "I'll cover you," he said, strategizing. "At the end of the mesa, there's an open spot. Four trails branch off from there. Take the one on the far left and head east. In a couple of miles, you'll find a temporary logging camp."

There was no time for questions. Without waiting for a reply, the shaman shoved Johns forward, unleashing a relentless barrage of gunfire, each shot crackling through the air like a thunderclap.

Johns and Zack sprinted through the underbrush, their feet pounding against the earth, adrenaline surging with every step. The sharp crack of gunshots echoed behind them, a deadly reminder the danger was far from over.

15

BREAKDOWN

SEDONA

Sarah watched the shaman's truck leave the parking lot and head east, farther into the Coconino Forest. She'd caught the look of disbelief in Johns' eyes when she told him she was not to go to the cave. She could hardly believe it herself when the shaman ordered her to stay behind. She had hoped for time alone with Dr. Johns to get answers to her vision that predicted his role regarding her failure to imagine a better world.

Sedona was less than a half-hour away. She planned to run into town and eat at her favorite restaurant, maybe even meet up briefly with one of her good friends who had a house in the city. As she drove, the Tesla's computer alarm chimed a warning. The screen indicated the battery charge was dropping rapidly. *Great,* she thought. Although Sedona lacked a Tesla dealership, it boasted a service center specializing in electric vehicles, complete with an emergency contact for weekends. The service wouldn't come cheap, but Sarah made the call. She pulled into their lot with her charge on zero.

The maintenance center included a Tesla supercharging station. While waiting for the mechanic, Sarah attempted to charge her vehicle but received another warning light. So, she called her friend and chatted for a while.

Eventually, Albie Milne, the owner of the service center, showed up. After a brief conversation, she drove into one of the repair bays. Inside the waiting room, Albie turned on the television for her then left for the repair bay. The ASU Sun Devils were playing the Kansas Jayhawks.

However, her attention was abruptly diverted by a breaking news banner announcing an explosion in the nearby Coconino Forest. As firefighters rushed to contain the ensuing blaze, Sarah stared at the location map, her concern mounting. "Damn, that's exactly where the guys were headed," she muttered, her worry intensifying. She immediately tried calling Zack, only to be directed to his voicemail, further fueling her anxiety.

Minutes later, Albie beckoned Sarah to follow him into the repair center. Reaching the elevated Tesla, he pointed to the small circular object attached to the underside. "You know what that is?"

Taken aback, Sarah shook her head.

"A GPS tracking device. Somebody's tracking you," Albie said, deepening Sarah's unease. "By the looks of it, it's NATO issue." He grinned, revealing two missing teeth. "I was stationed in Heidelberg for two years. Motor Pool. My unit worked with the German forces. That's how I know about this. All the German trucks were equipped with these trackers."

"Fucking great," Sarah swore.

Albie frowned. "Sorry, but that's not the bad news."

News worse than someone tracking my movements? Sarah kept the anger and dismay off her face. "What else?"

"I can't figure out what's happening with the battery circuits. There's a Tesla expert in town, but he won't be available until tomorrow morning."

Sarah nodded. "I guess that'll have to do."

Sarah's phone vibrated. Caller ID said Zack. "I need to take this."

As she turned to go outside, the mechanic asked, "What do you want me to do about the tracking device?"

"Leave it for now." She stalked out of the maintenance bay and put her phone to her ear. "You and Johns okay?"

"Barely," the filmmaker replied. Zack's rushed story of a gunman chasing them cut off abruptly as the signal dropped.

Albie followed her out of the bay and listened to her side of the conversation. When the call ended, he leaned against the wall and stared at the horizon, where the sun hung a handbreadth above the trees. "Everything all right?" he asked, wiping his hands with an oily rag.

"Nothing is ever all right these days," Sarah replied, her frustration boiling out through her tone.

"Ain't that the truth. World seems headed toward disaster every freakin' minute." He grinned, his missing front teeth making him look like a meth head. "You have a place to stay?"

"I do."

"Okay. I'll call you tomorrow when the specialist gets here."

"Thanks." Sarah made another call.

16

TEMPORARY LOGGING CAMP

COCONINO FOREST

Behind Zack and Johns, a ball of fire erupted into the sky, an ominous, roaring blaze that mushroomed upward, casting a fiery glow over the darkening forest. Moments later, the blast wave slammed into them and Johns was thrown forward, crashing hard onto the rocky path. His arms instinctively shot out to break the fall, but the impact jarred his shoulders painfully. Zack, desperate to save his camera, twisted mid-stumble and smashed against a boulder, wrenching his ankle in the process.

Dazed and battered, they scrambled to their feet and watched the fireball devour the last light of the setting sun. Its eerie glow cast an otherworldly incandescence across the landscape.

"That came from the cave!" Zack shouted.

"The shaman!" Johns groaned, his voice heavy with despair. "He must be dead."

Zack grimaced, his voice shaky. "Yeah... maybe," he muttered, though neither man wanted to accept the possibility. The shaman had been their guide, their protector—and now, he might be gone. Zack tested his ankle, wincing, and found it could still hold his weight. "We better keep moving. We can't let the guy with the rifle catch up."

Johns nodded grimly.

The crackling thunder of burning forest reached them and they gasped at the transformed tree line, the sky a horrifying blend of night and fire.

"This way!" Johns shouted, and with Zack limping behind him, they pressed on eastward, each step a struggle against mounting exhaustion. The fiery glow in the west lit up the forest, casting flickering shadows that made it easier for Johns to stay on the trail, but the devastation behind them gnawed at his mind.

"You know where you're going?" Zack asked, his voice strained and doubt filled.

Johns tried to stay focused. "The shaman told us to take the leftmost trail and follow it to a logging camp. I just hope he was right."

A heavy silence settled between them, broken only by their labored breaths. The cold of the evening crept in, biting at their skin, pushing them to quicken their pace. With each limp and stumble, the weight of their situation bore down on them, the uncertainty of survival hanging in the air like the smoke from the distant fire.

Then remarkably, Zack's phone pinged. They had a signal! Zack called Sarah and tried to tell her what happened to them, but the signal dropped immediately. They hiked on. The evening grew colder, and Zack's ankle ached more now that the adrenaline had worn off.

Up ahead, a light appeared in the dark. They stopped, wondering if the man who blew up the cave had flown ahead of them and waited in ambush. But the light did not move, and they quickly realized it wasn't from a flashlight, but an overhead light, perhaps a streetlamp, offering a beacon of hope and a possible end to their harrowing escape.

The two men wove between an outer ring of logs piled in tall triangular prisms and entered a logging camp. A giant Track Harvester loomed like a behemoth from a horror film. An office trailer sat in the middle of the clearing, bathed in the glow of a solar powered mercury vapor lamp, its stark white lines silhouetted sharply. The happy coincidence of their refuge relieved the exhausted men. Temporary logging operations like this were designed to mitigate fire risks and now offered them sanctuary.

After their narrow escape from the mysterious shooter and explosion, a blanket of quiet shock enveloped both men. Zack grappled with the trauma of their death-defying experience, while Johns wrestled with the realization his old life now seemed meaningless.

In the momentary safety of the logging camp, Zack asked, "What's going on here? This isn't the documentary project I was hired to do."

"As the rabbi said, 'Unless you have ears to hear and unless you have eyes to see, what is going on cannot be understood by the masses.'"

"What the hell does that mean?" Zack shouted, frustration and confusion boiling over.

"Sorry, that just came out. I ... umm ... since my wife died, these kinds of things pop into my mind out of the blue, and sometimes I say them out loud."

"What now?"

"Do we have cell service?"

Zack pulled out his phone "We do."

"Make a call to Sarah, for starters, and I'll check out the trailer."

Miraculously, the office door swung open, so Johns went inside. In one corner, a small desk held maps and notes. Overalls dangled from hooks against one wall, and cases of bottled water were stacked beside a desk scarred by cigarette burns.

Exhausted and thirsty, he drained two of the small bottles before grabbing a third and holding it close to his heart with his eyes closed, as if performing a ritual. His mind quieted unexpectedly. Then, pulling out the votive relief from his backpack, he studied it. The two raised eyes stared back at him from across space and time, stirring a newfound sense of purpose within him.

It dawned on him—a paper written by a colleague, Gerald Gunderson, argued that the imagery on the tablet represented the eyeless vision of a nonphysical body associated with near-death experiences.

The moment of revelation ended as Zack pounded the side of the trailer. "You in there, Isaac?" he yelled.

Placing the Eye back in his pack, Johns walked out of the trailer and found Zack leaning heavily against the side. "You okay, man?"

"Yeah, just this ankle, and I'm tired and thirsty."

Johns threw him the water bottle. "Here. There's more inside." He disappeared and returned a moment later with three more bottles of water. Zack had already drained the first one. "So did you get a hold of Sarah?"

Zack chugged another half bottle. "I told her everything that happened and pinged our location. She's staying with a friend; something happened to her Tesla. The road to our location is blocked off because of the fire. They'll try to get us out in the morning. She said her friend has some answers for us about what happened."

"We can sleep on the floor inside. There's lots of water, a first aid kit, and emergency blankets."

"Sounds good." Zack pulled open the zipper in his fanny pack.

"What've you got in there?"

"Extra SD cards, a solid-state two-terabyte hard drive, and most importantly a battery charging pack." He handed his phone and the battery pack to Johns. "Charge our phones; we'll need the flashlights once it gets totally dark."

"What are you going to do?"

"Copy the camera footage to the hard drive for you to keep. Whatever was in that cave was important enough to film, so we should have backups."

"Always the filmmaker," Johns teased, a slight smile breaking through the confusion and disbelief of their surreal predicament.

"If we get out of here alive, I'm done with this shit."

17

CYNTHIA APPLE
SEDONA

Cynthia Apple picked up Sarah in her hybrid Range Rover. Though she was in her early seventies, she looked twenty years younger, with penetrating green eyes and dark brown hair. She held an emeritus professorship of philosophy at Rice University, specializing in the philosophy of technology. Rumor stated she consulted with NASA and knew more about the technology of traveling into space than many of the engineers at the Lyndon B. Johnson Space Center outside of Houston, Texas. She also held several profitable patents used in the aerospace program, which was how she met Sarah's father.

After Sarah took one of Cynthia's seminars at Rice, they developed a meaningful mentorship. Like her father, Sarah possessed an intuitive grasp of technological complexity, and Cynthia expressed surprise she had not taken her talents to the marketplace of artificial intelligence but instead chose to work with nonprofits to bring more women into politics.

As Cynthia drove to her home in one of Sedona's wealthier neighborhoods, she sensed Sarah's distress. "So sorry about your father. I can't imagine the trauma of having him killed right in front of you."

"Thanks. It was—" Sarah let the thought go unfinished.

"You poor kid. Losing a parent is never easy, but this…how are you doing?"

"Some days are harder than others, but I'm okay."

"I'd imagine." Cynthia glanced at her then back to the road. "Your dad and I were quite close."

"I know. He always spoke of you with great admiration."

Cynthia pulled into a wide drive that arced in front of a southwest-style adobe home. Junipers and manzanita trees bordered the narrow portico entrance. "Let's get inside, and we can talk more."

The spacious house was decorated with a rich blend of Native American and Spanish influences. Natural materials incorporating warm earthy tones, and rustic textures created an inviting and comfortable atmosphere.

A big bay window looked out on the chapel of the Holy Cross.

While Cynthia poured two glasses of wine, Sarah sat quietly in one of the heavy wood and leather chairs.

Cynthia handed Sarah a glass of Pinot Grigio and sat in the chair opposite her. "Your grief for your father aside, I can see something else is wrong, more than the battery failure of your Tesla."

Sarah twisted in her chair and looked out at the chapel. The sun's dying rays reflected off the red rock buttes behind, engulfing the chapel in a lurid red. "There is, but I can't talk about it."

"You can. It's about the explosion at the cave."

Sarah took a deep breath. Cynthia had always been a strange one. So totally present with each person while at the same time impenetrable herself. Sarah accepted the rumors about Dr. Apple's successes outside of the university were true.

She leaned forward. "How do you know the explosion was at the cave?"

Cynthia smiled in a way indicating she was asking the right question. "In the same way you know about future events. You and I, we share impossible skills."

"So, you know about the cave?"

"I only know it's nearby, somewhere along the ley line that runs through Sedona. I could never see it; the exact location was blocked. But after the explosion, I clearly saw the man who set the charge."

"Do you know what our plan was?"

"No, please tell me."

With relief, Sarah unburdened herself by talking about all that happened after her father was murdered.

Cynthia listened wholeheartedly as she was brought up to date. "Who is this ancient Greek expert who knows about the Eleusis Mysteries?"

"Professor Isaac Johns from Yale."

Shaken by the name Sarah uttered, Cynthia went to the minibar and poured another glass of wine. Sitting down again, she said, "I was part of Dr. Johns' wife's doctoral committee. She was also taking a remote viewing class when she died in that tragic accident."

Sarah's mind raced. "Are they connected—the class and my father's death?"

"I never found out, dear. On the other hand," Cynthia waved the wineglass at her room and its furnishings, "I don't believe in useless coincidences; synchronicities are another matter."

Sarah had many more questions, but a call from Zack interrupted. She listened intently as he described their circumstances. "Send me the coordinates." Immediately, her phone pinged with the location.

Cynthia pulled out her phone "Forward it to me, and I'll find out where they are." Within moments Cynthia mapped the location and found the Forest Service road leading to the logging camp. "We can't get there tonight. The fire has blocked off a large section of the road."

Sarah nodded. "Zack, the best road into your area is blocked because of the fire." Zack's expletive could be heard without the speaker. Sarah grimaced. "If we find another route or the road is reopened, I might be able to pick you up in the morning. I'll call you."

Zack thanked her and she said goodbye.

Setting the phone down, she asked Cynthia, "Is there something we can do? Report this to the authorities?"

"The Forest Service has already responded to the fire, and no one else can get through to them, at present." She squeezed Sarah's hand in reassurance. "They're going to be fine."

Cynthia crossed to the big bay window, pondering a decision she needed to make. Sitting back in the chair, she said, "There's something you need to know."

Sarah didn't wait for Cynthia to begin. "Who was the Indian guide who wouldn't let me travel to the cave? There was something unreal about him."

"The shaman is not real, but at the same time is the most real. He … she … they are a kind of spiritual guide. In near-death experiences, they are the clear light. That which connects all humanity to the one."

Sarah knew about theories of "the one"—the divine connecting all humans. "How do you know him?"

"I met him on my trip to the cave."

The admission surprised Sarah. "I thought you said you weren't able to remote view the cave."

"Not this cave, the first one."

"I'm not following."

"My dear Sarah, you are an integral part of a grand experiment in human evolution."

This echoed her father's esoteric predictions too much to be coincidence. "What are you keeping from me?"

"Not now. This needs to wait until I meet Dr. Johns."

18

—————

DARK SKIES

SEDONA

Sedona called itself a dark sky city, dedicated to preserving the sanctity of the night sky. The lack of significant outdoor lighting made the service center specializing in electric vehicles little more than a dark shapeless blob among darker shadows.

The irony of the situation wasn't lost on Janus Snyder as he parked in his Tesla Cybertruck across from the darkened service station waiting for Sarah Davenport to return for her vehicle. Although Snyder hated the meaninglessness of the technological world he found himself embedded in, its latest advances inexplicably drew him, so he surrounded himself with them despite his disdain. This paradox gripped him: loathing the technologies that fascinated him, unable to escape the allure of progress even as it represented everything he despised.

He'd had an exhausting day. The brief firefight with a man who eerily resembled his father clouded his mind to the point he lost his balance and fell. When he regained his perch, the man had vanished. After setting the charges to seal the new Eleusinian cave for good, he and Turk raced back to the helicopter. The fire ignited by the explosion provided enough distraction for him to escape undetected. What puzzled him most when he reached the helicopter was that the truck was gone. How could this old man have returned so quickly?

Snyder slept for an hour. Upon waking, the moon cast enough light for him to spot a security camera on the front of the building. He decided to act instead of wait. In addition to being a dark sky city, Sedona boasted a city-wide internet portal. Within seconds, Snyder's skills enabled him to hack into the camera's feed and download stored video files.

On the retrieved footage, Sarah drove her Tesla into the repair bay, walked outside to talk on the phone, and then returned inside. The last bit of footage showed her getting into a Range Rover with a woman driving. Snyder entered the license plate number into a dark web hacker site. It didn't take long for someone from the community to inform him the SUV belonged to Cynthia Apple.

Snyder's phone vibrated, signaling the presence of his contact. The man on the other end sounded annoyed. "You made quite a mess, starting a fire and everything. Were you able to complete your mission and obtain the Eye?"

Annoyed by the man's tone, Snyder replied, "There was no fucking Greek eye, and I looked everywhere."

"That's disappointing. What about the two men?"

"They escaped. Some old man helped them."

A long silence followed. "What are you doing now?"

"I'm waiting for Sarah Davenport to pick up her Tesla. When I put the tracker on her car, I also partially disabled her charging system."

"Where is she now?"

"She was picked up by a woman, Cynthia Apple."

Another long pause followed. "There is a change of plans; just back off for now."

"I don't like being messed with." Snyder angrily disconnected and turned his phone off. *I know someone who will have answers.*

19

A TURNING POINT

SEDONA

After Sarah went to bed, Cynthia sat on her porch, watching the dim glow of the fire diminish. She was organizing in her mind how much to reveal to Sarah and Johns. Her phone buzzed. Startled by who was on the other end, she pushed the answer button.

"Is Sarah Davenport with you?"

"Surprisingly, yes," Cynthia replied. "I thought your man would take care of everything."

"There was an unexpected interference."

"I heard. The shaman."

"The plan has changed."

Cynthia listened intently for two minutes as her caller explained the new plan, and then replied, "Will do."

20

THE PROMETHEUS PROJECT – ORIGIN

COCONINO NATIONAL FOREST ROAD

My name is Gerald Gunderson, and I was tasked with documenting what became known as the Prometheus Project.

"Who is this Gunderson?" Sarah asked, pulling her gaze from the paper Cynthia had handed to her as they drove east toward the Forest Service road that led to the temporary logging camp where Johns and Zack waited to be rescued.

"Read on," Cynthia answered. "Your questions will be answered."

Sarah turned back to the paper:

The Judean Desert, home to over 800 caves, including the renowned Qumran Caves where the Dead Sea Scrolls were discovered in the 1940s and 1950s, played a pivotal role in our understanding of ancient texts.

By the summer of 1947, Jerusalem was entrenched in a bitter division between Arabs and Jews. During this tumultuous period, Metropolitan Samuel learned of what would be known as the Dead Sea Scrolls, subsequently securing them for his possession. Upon acquiring the Hebrew manuscripts, Metropolitan Samuel promptly dispatched one of his priests, accompanied by a merchant, to verify the cave's location as indicated by the Bedouins.

Their exploration confirmed the existence of the cave, unveiling jars, fragments of linen wrappings, and pieces of scrolls. Later, a Bedouin revealed to Samuel the location of another cave purportedly of greater significance to Christianity containing a well-preserved scroll and a stone Greek icon colloquially called "the Eye." Despite Metropolitan Samuel sending a trusted relative to investigate, the artifacts were ultimately transported to the United States by the relative, Mar Samuel, instead of returned.

The four scrolls brought to the United States are among the earliest to be discovered in late 1946 or early 1947. It emerged that Mar Samuel, also known as Archbishop Samuel, had knowledge of the original Eye icon and the scroll detailing Jesus's near-death experience during the time he wandered the wilderness subsequent to his baptism by John. During his time at Duke University, Samuel introduced Dr. Arturo Rosenblueth to the existence of the Eye and the scroll. Between 1951 and 1952, with funding from the Rockefeller Foundation, Rosenblueth acquired these items from Samuel. Rosenblueth then returned to Harvard to collaborate with Norbert Wiener on deciphering the scrolls, recognizing the potential for a medical procedure that could unlock humanity's greatest potential.

The scrolls detailed an initiation ceremony, and the use of a substance thought to be akin to that used in the Eleusinian Mysteries, speculated by Marvin Minsky to be similar to LSD. In the mid-1960s, supported once again by the Rockefeller Foundation, a group of young engineers from MIT and Stanford, including myself, constructed the first cave in Pinnacles National Monument to conduct the most ambitious experiment: becoming gods.

The Metropolitan Samuel scroll outlined a precise set of procedures: a clearing chant, a combination of a sedative and

LSD, and at the moment of sleep, the initiate would be compelled to peer through the Eye into the vast universe of all knowledge.

Each initiate was accompanied by one or two members of the Prometheus Project and occasionally a mysterious shamanic guide. Early participants included industry leaders such as Thomas Watson Jr., Bill Hewlett, Gordon Moore, and Marvin Minsky, who leveraged their experiences to drive the AI and computer revolution.

However, transhumanists like Marvin Minsky dedicated themselves to life extension and mind enhancement technologies. Given the technological advancements of the past half-century, the human body's limited mental capacities had become obsolete. Other initiates developed superhuman abilities, including clairvoyance, remote viewing, telepathic communication, and telekinetic healing, becoming respected mediums.

The Prometheus Project was conducted with the utmost secrecy; most participants were unaware of the others' identities. The project was eventually discovered when a hiker stumbled upon the cave in Pinnacles National Park, but the situation was quickly contained after convincing the hiker what they had witnessed was merely a sophisticated joke. The project was suspended until the 1990s, when near-death experiences became widely documented by the medical community.

Sarah checked the spidery scrawl at the bottom of the last page—Gerald Gunderson, San Jose, California, 2023. She took in a deep breath to settle the nerves in her stomach. "Is this true?"

21

THE NEW PLAN

COCONINO NATIONAL FOREST ROAD

Cynthia pulled the Range Rover to a stop on the side of the Forest Service road. The sun had climbed above the Coconino National Forest during the fifteen minutes it took Sarah to read and reread the Xeroxed monograph, committing parts of it to memory. As she finished, a mix of shock and reluctant understanding settled over her—somehow, she had sensed this all along. She handed the paper to Cynthia, who pulled a lighter from the pocket of her multi-colored vest and set the monograph on fire. Rolling down the window, Cynthia held the burning paper by the fingertips of her left hand until the flames consumed it. She let the ashes flutter away then stepped out of the car to grind them into the gravel berm.

Cynthia climbed back into the car. She leaned forward. "I bet you're asking yourself what the chances were five days ago that we would be here right now talking about the key roles we are all about to play in the future of the human species."

"Looking back now, it almost seems preordained, at least since my father was murdered," Sarah mused.

"Yes, but it's not anything you're doing."

"I don't understand."

"Neuroscience clearly demonstrates the brain produces the feeling, the sense, that you're an agent in the world, and that you're in charge of what you're doing. The first thing that happens during an NDE is realizing this sense of self is a creation to navigate the ever-changing flow of life long enough to survive and reproduce."

A moment of great realization struck Sarah. "Of course, my dad always loved quoting, 'You must die before you die to become immortal.'"

"He was right, of course," Cynthia affirmed.

"What happened with Phase Two?"

"After we pick up the boys, you'll be able to ask Gerald Gunderson himself."

"How is that possible?"

"You're going to San Jose."

Sarah widened her eyes. "My God, you're involved in this whole thing."

"Your dad would want you to trust me. Can you do that?"

Sarah unbuckled her seat belt and stepped out of the car. The acrid scent of smoke and charred wood lingered in the air, settling uneasily over the forest. Though the eastern edge of yesterday's wildfire was contained, sparing the logging camp where Zack and Johns had holed up, an uneasy tension clung to Sarah like the smoke itself. She walked to the rear of the vehicle, scanning the road behind them, her gut telling her they were being followed. But even that gnawing fear couldn't compete with the storm raging inside her—her fear and anger at being manipulated, swept into a conspiracy she barely understood yet somehow knew she had always been destined to be part of.

Cynthia wasn't the only one to draw her into the Prometheus Project. Her father played a role too, along with others whose intentions were shrouded in mystery. Her mind churned with the weight of it all, the feeling of being a pawn in someone else's game. But underneath that anger, a deeper knowing tugged at her consciousness. Part of her—something she couldn't quite put into words—had always sensed she was meant to be here. Not just as a participant, but as something more. This plan had been in motion long before she ever knew about the project. A strange sense of familiarity with the unfolding events made her question her role. Was she merely a victim of the Prometheus Project, or had she been its architect all along?

The thought startled her. Her instinct told her to demand Cynthia turn the car around and drive back to Sedona. She wanted to walk away, to leave all of this behind. But as the sun cleared the last of the trees, casting a warm, golden light over the landscape, something inside her shifted. The light burned away the fog in her mind, leaving only clarity. She blinked against the brightness, and in that moment, she knew the truth. From the moment she'd left the Las Vegas convention center in the chaotic aftermath of her father's murder, she had been seeking answers. Those answers were at last within her reach.

She thought again of the numbers her father gave her before he died—1162413. They were the key, the missing piece of the puzzle. Somehow, they would unlock everything.

With a deep breath, Sarah slid back into the passenger seat. Her hands were steady now, her mind focused. "For now," she said.

22

JOHNS MAKES A CALL
LOGGING CAMP, COCONINO FOREST

Isaac Johns woke cold in the lumber camp's office, stomach tight with excitement and fear. Fate had propelled him into a series of events that seemed impossible a few days ago. His old friend snored softly across the room, head cradled in the crook of his left arm. Dungarees covered him from head to toe. Johns, careful not to make any noise, rose and left the trailer.

Outside, smoke colored the air, turning dawn into a red slash above the trees to the east. His breath formed clouds around his face, and he pulled the windbreaker tighter around himself against the autumn chill. In the distance a lone coyote bayed, its doleful cry echoing mournfully against the ebbing night.

Johns never felt more confused in his life. He missed his wife and wished he could tell her what was happening to get her perspective on what to do next.

He imagined her voice and the coy little smile she gave when tweaking his indecisiveness. "Isaac, do the simple things first then the bigger decisions will follow." For a few minutes, he felt compelled to join her, but something was telling him not now.

Johns pulled his cell phone from the jacket pocket and punched in the number for Gary Kerzner, the post-doc working with him on his lectures for the seminar at Arizona State University. The young man's sleepy voice answered on the third ring. "I'm here, Professor. What do you need?"

Johns chuckled to himself, imagining the post-doc's censored sentiment—*what does that idiot want at this ungodly hour?*

"Gary, I need you to fill in for me at the talk tomorrow night."

"Shit, doc, I'm … I'm totally unprepared."

"This is your chance to be recognized, Gary. You've been doing the heavy lifting on our research for the past semester. You can do it."

The sound of the young man swallowing was audible over the phone. "Yes, sir … I will, sir. How long will you be away?"

Johns paused for a moment. He had no idea what would come next. "At least a week. Make the arguments to the group you proposed to me last week." He hung up. *That was the easy one. Now for the "I don't know what the fuck's going to happen next" call.*

He went through the phone's contacts. Under "Eleusinian" was a single name and a single phone number he was warned not to call unless it was an emergency. *Strange shamans … being shot at … explosions … forest fire … I think those qualify as an emergency.* He checked the time—6:37. *It's the same time in California,* he reminded himself and dialed.

"Dr. Gunderson," he said when the party answered.

"Dr. Johns," the voice clipped in with a slight Midwest accent. "I was hoping you would call."

The old guy expected an emergency. Johns forced his voice to remain calm. "I think it's time we talked about Eleusis and NDEs."

"Indeed. How soon can you get here?"

The sound of a car engine cut through the silence. Johns judged it to be a mile away. *Probably not the killer. Must be Sarah and her friend.* "A couple of days. I'm in Arizona."

"Good. Give me a call when you're a couple of hours out from San Jose, and I'll tell you where we will meet. By the way, I never got a PhD like you did." The phone went dead.

Johns pocketed his phone and turned to face the approaching vehicle. Sarah was in the passenger seat, and he sighed with relief.

23

ESCAPE

MOJAVE DESERT

The drive from Sedona to Zach's cabin near Lucerne Valley, California, took seven hours following the I-40 route.

"Will Zack be okay?" Sarah asked Johns.

He nodded, staring at the San Bernardino Mountains.

"Are you sure?" she persisted, trying to draw him out. He'd been quiet since they'd dropped Zack off at his cabin.

Johns turned toward her. "Only three people know his cabin exists, and that includes you and me. It's in the middle of nowhere, completely off the grid. Solar power, a well taps the aquifer, self-composting toilet, 128-bit encryption link to a satellite server. He's safer than we are." Johns grimaced and went back to watching the scenery, recalling how Cynthia had insisted on a new wardrobe for everyone before they departed Sedona.

* * *

"You can't stay in Sedona," Cynthia admonished the trio after rescuing Johns and Zack from the logging camp. They stopped outside a used clothing and gear shop in Sedona. "You'll need new clothes, gear, burner phones."

"New identities?" Zack quipped.

"We haven't time for those. You'll just have to keep a low profile."

"Sounds serious, like a Jason Bourne novel."

"The man hunting you tried to kill you and blew up the cave to cover his tracks. Is that serious enough for you?" Cynthia said acidly.

Zack nodded meekly and went to the men's large section for clothes.

Outside the store, they packed Cynthia's Range Rover with everything they'd need for a cross-country trip. She handed Sarah the keys. "Stay off the main roads and camp when you stop. No motels ... no credit cards," she ordered.

"You're not coming with us?" Sarah asked.

"No, dear. Someone has to return your rental so the man following you thinks you're still in the area. Besides, I haven't been to Phoenix in a long time."

"What'll we do for money?" Zack asked.

Cynthia handed Sarah an envelope stuffed with hundred-dollar bills. "That should be enough to tide you over. Tell Gerald Gunderson I said hello, and for heaven sakes keep the Eye safe." She went back into the store.

* * *

The drive was becoming monotonous, so Sarah turned to Johns. "What's your take on Cynthia's explanation about why they stopped bringing initiates to the cave? That they bungled their childhood probe into Bob Smith, so post-initiation he spiraled into madness before embarking on a murderous frenzy?"

Johns exhaled deeply. His fingers deftly summoned information on his phone. "I delved into what happened online. The story is horrifying. Seems as if Bob Smith was a protégé of Dr. Alvarez, toiling away in the medical engineering lab at Stanford. It says he came perilously close to ending the professor's life then unleashed a copycat rampage across Nebraska, tracing the path Charles Stark-weather blazed in 1958. He even mimicked James Dean's look. Here's where it gets interesting. When he was apprehended, Smith proclaimed himself a deity, an immortal, shouting apocalyptic visions of the world engulfed in flames."

"So, this could hint at a more sinister aspect to Prometheus Project?" Sarah asked.

Johns nodded.

"And what of Cynthia's dread? That Smith remains a dormant volcano, poised to divulge the cave's secrets and the medically induced near-death experiences to any open ear?"

"Her fears track, but it also seems she's harboring secrets about Smith."

"You suggest he's like me?"

"Possibly."

Silence enveloped them as they continued their journey, the atmosphere heavy with unspoken thoughts.

After a moment, Johns, his voice trembling with emotion, said quietly, "There's a part of my life I've never shared with anyone." His eyes, glistening, lifted toward the sky as if seeking solace. "I was with Helene as she left this world. What I experienced is something called a shared death experience."

He paused, his breath catching. "I wasn't just in that hospital room anymore. Suddenly, I was outside it, free. I saw Helene... but she wasn't alone. She was with our son. Our beautiful boy—he died two days after he was born. His body was too fragile, his organs underdeveloped... he never had a chance. But in that moment, I saw him. I knew him. We both—Helene and I—wrapped him in love. Love we couldn't give him in life."

Johns' voice wavered, the weight of memory pressing down on him. "It was so pure, so beautiful. And we were together, all of us, for that one perfect moment. Then they both moved toward the light, to that place people talk about—the tunnel. And I stayed behind. I wanted to go with them."

His voice broke; tears streamed down his face, the grief raw and uncontainable. Sarah, unable to find words to match the weight of what he had just shared, rested her hand gently on his shoulder. Her touch was a silent vow of understanding, a shared acknowledgment of the pain no words could ease. His heart might be breaking, yet beneath that grief, his strength, his love, transcended the unbearable loss.

She gripped the steering wheel with renewed determination, driving forward into the unknown. Every mile, every second, brought them closer to the truth she desperately sought, each heartbeat entwined with the depth of his revelation.

24

TIME SLIP

JOKHANG TEMPLE, LHASA, TIBET

Nestled in the heart of Lhasa, Tibet, the Jokhang Temple had for over a thousand years been revered as one of the most sacred temples in Tibetan Buddhism. Its foundations were laid in the seventh century by King Songtsen Gampo, the temple designed to enshrine the precious Buddha statues brought by his foreign brides: Princess Wencheng of the Chinese Tang dynasty and Princess Bhrikuti of Nepal. As centuries passed, the temple expanded to cover approximately 25,000 square meters. Its architecture, a harmonious blend of Indian vihara design with Tibetan and Nepalese elements, mirrored the rich cultural interplay within Tibet.

The Jokhang Temple held a special place in the hearts of Tibetan Buddhists as the ultimate pilgrimage destination. It was home to the Jowo Rinpoche—a life-sized statue representing Buddha at the age of twelve, revered above all others in Tibetan Buddhism. Hidden from the public, within the temple, a small room contained the bones believed to belong to Siddhartha Gautama, the Buddha Shakyamuni, positioned in the timeless lotus pose.

Forty years ago in this room, Gerald Gunderson met with the temple's head Rinpoche in an extraordinary encounter. Gunderson, with his youthful taut wiry frame and balding, Scandinavian round head, bowed to the lama and asked him about time slips. Their meeting was outwardly silent, an exchange of thoughts through telepathy rather than spoken words.

The Rinpoche shared his unique experience with Gunderson, revealing he had encountered his first time slip in the 1930s as a young boy. He was taught by his mentors how to navigate these temporal anomalies, claiming, in a spiritual sense, to be over 130 years old. Both shared a moment of understanding, marked by a respectful bow and an exchange of smiles.

Then the Rinpoche confided in Gunderson about meeting Cynthia in 1977. "When she arrived at the temple gates, I saw immediately she was experiencing time slips. Within two days, I was able to teach her how to control them. Ever since then, this has been her sanctuary to merge with the one."

Gerald Gunderson smiled at the memory of his first meeting with the Rinpoche and the startling revelation that time slips existed. Forty years later, time slips had become second nature to him. Breathing deeply, he closed his eyes. When he opened them again, Cynthia and General Davidson, dressed in a Space Force uniform, were also present in the small interior room of the Jokhang Temple.

"I've never gotten used to these time slips," the general mused. "It goes against everything I've learned about space and time. How is it possible that everything at Vandenberg, Sedona, and San Jose stands still as we carry on a conversation in the sacred temple for what, ten … fifteen minutes?"

"Perhaps it's because you had a natural near-death experience, unlike the induced ones Cynthia and I had."

Their minds momentarily merged into a single entity, a process that unveiled a critical insight to all three—Johns held the Eye and was destined to play a key role in their plan.

The entity split back into three individual minds.

Cynthia asked, "When is the rocket launch?"

The general looked at his watch. "Two days, supposedly. We still don't know the chant or where the new cave is."

The other two nodded in agreement.

Their minds cohered one more time back into consensus space and time. Together, they focused their unique energies to precipitate the success of Johns and Sarah in bringing about the goal of the Prometheus Project.

As their collective consciousness aligned and then returned to individual awareness, they found themselves firmly rooted once again in the ordinary reality of space and time.

25

DESERT ECHOES
MOJAVE DESERT

Zack sat in the single chair beside the large table that dominated the cabin's rustic interior. A simple cot against the far wall was his bed. The bathroom had no door, and the sink doubled for dishes. A portable electric cooler served as a refrigerator. Beside it, on a plywood counter, a Coleman stove boiled water for tea. Aside from the open door, four windows, one in each wall, let in the harsh desert light. A kerosene heater provided the only warmth on those infrequent nights when the desert's temperature fell below freezing.

The kettle whistled loudly, jerking Zack out of the torpor that invaded his body after surviving the events at the cave and the harrowing night in the logging camp trailer. He rose unsteadily, his ankle still hurting, and grabbed the back of the chair for support, before moving to the makeshift kitchen. Pulling an Earl Grey tea tin from the cupboard, he scooped a generous amount into the teapot, added water and set it aside. He set the timer on his watch for five minutes and waited, watching the desert's afternoon light playing against the yuccas, Joshua trees, and cholla.

The watch timer interrupted his reverie. He poured the Earl Grey into a large mug and added a teaspoon of sugar. He checked his watch again and started in surprise. An hour had passed since Johns and Sarah dropped him at his personal oasis. "Fuck! Get ahold of yourself," he said aloud.

Going outside, Zack sat on the bench tucked beneath an overhang beside the front door and fixed his gaze on the giant Joshua tree that stood sentinel on his property. The yucca's gnarled and twisted limbs had always been a source of comfort and clarity for him. After several minutes his thoughts steadied, and he knew what he had to do. He powered on his third-generation portable Starlink system, punched a number into his phone, and waited,

A voice message greeted him: "This is Sam Hill. Leave a message."

"This is Zack Helm. Call me immediately."

It took less than a minute for Zack's phone to vibrate with an incoming call.

"Zack, good to hear from you. How are you doing? How did the shoot go?" Sam's voice on the other end was casual, as though he were oblivious to what happened.

"Bastard! You set me up. I nearly got killed."

"Wait, what happened?"

Zack's anger escalated. "Don't play dumb with me, you son of a bitch. This was never about a series."

"Zack, calm down. You got your money, right?"

"I'm waiting on the wire transfer for the rest."

"The rest of the fifty grand will be in your account tomorrow after you deliver the files. I presume you managed to film the cave?"

"Of course I did. The footage is right here in my camera. But let me make this clear—it's going to cost you more than fifty grand. I want serious answers."

"How—"

"Shut up. I'll call you when I'm ready... and Sam? Go to hell."

Zack ended the call and seethed, staring out into the desolate expanse of the Mojave, where secrets and betrayals stretched as endless as the desert itself.

26

DAD SPEAKS

CALIFORNIA CENTRAL VALLEY

Sarah gripped the wheel as the desert landscape blurred by. In the passenger seat, Johns hunched over the glow of the laptop screen reflecting his intense gaze. He barely acknowledged Sarah's presence, offering nothing more than the occasional grunt or a distracted shake of his head whenever she attempted conversation.

Frustrated, Sarah finally pulled the SUV over to the side of the road. "Your turn to drive," she said, her voice firm, eyes fixed on him.

Johns blinked, momentarily pulled from the depths of the cave footage. He followed her out of the car, and together they stood beside the vehicle, staring at the surreal landscape. Towering rows of olive-colored Joshua trees stretched before them, their otherworldly gnarled branches clawing at the sky.

His voice cut through the quiet, low and enigmatic. "Very biblical... fitting, really. Early settlers believed these trees looked like the Israelite leader Joshua raising his arms, guiding them to the promised land."

Sarah frowned, intrigued but puzzled. "How is it biblical? What do you mean?"

Johns turned to her, eyes narrowed in thought. "Isn't that what we're doing, in a sense?"

Sarah raised an eyebrow, still not following. "I don't understand."

He paused, the desert wind brushing past them as he weighed his next words. "The symbols in that cave—they're pointing us to a promised land, something hidden. There's a code embedded in those markings. I just need to figure it out."

His words hung in the air, thick with mystery. For the first time that day, Sarah sensed more behind Johns' obsession than mere curiosity. A deepening connection joined them now—an unspoken understanding they were both on the brink of something much larger than either of them had anticipated.

They returned to the vehicle, a quiet intensity settling between them. As Johns climbed into the driver's seat and revved the engine, Sarah asked softly, "Can I use your headphones?"

Johns handed them to her, and the quiet exchange felt more intimate than before. As the SUV sped back onto the road, Sarah plugged the data stick Cynthia had given her into the laptop and slipped on the headphones.

Her breath caught as the screen flickered to life. Her father stared back at her, his familiar face set in the stern expression he always wore during his lectures about trusting her instincts. He was sitting in his office at the Johnson Space Center, and though the clip was clearly recorded years ago, the weight of his words still felt immediate, like a message sent across time—one meant for her, now, in this moment.

"I can't tell you how much I love you and always have. But if you're watching this, it means you're part of the Prometheus Project, and I'm probably dead for the second time.

"In the mid-1980s, I was a computer engineer working at IBM as they entered the market with a personal computer. I was part of the team tasked with working with Microsoft to adopt its operating system, PC DOS. I was approached by a high-level executive at Microsoft—I won't say who—and asked if I would be interested in participating in an experimental and highly secret program to enhance cognitive performance. Of course, I jumped at the opportunity, considering who was asking.

"At the time, Dr. Raymond Moody had just come out with his book on near-death experiences, which I immediately read thoroughly. This kind of transformational experience was new to me, but if what he claimed was true, NDEs are the most powerful event that has occurred throughout history. What I was told was that a group of people had developed a method for producing medically-induced NDEs. There were risks involved, but I felt an intuitive urgency to participate.

"Three years later, I was taken to a well-hidden cave north of Silicon Valley by two members of the Prometheus Project. When we entered the cave, one of the people, a lovely young woman, began a chant, which she said originated when consciousness first arose in humanity's evolution.

"Immediately, the energy level of my body rose, as did my level of conscious awareness. Later, this experience was described to me as a kundalini awakening. When it reached its zenith, I was handed an ancient Greek sculpture called the Eye. When I looked into it, my mind emptied, and I was absorbed into the vastness of the cosmos. The project leaders injected me with what I believe was ketamine. Almost immediately, I started dying. But it seemed perfectly okay.

"What happened next is hard to describe. I clearly remember floating above my body, which was lying on a bed. The people who had brought me to the cave seemed concerned about my well-being. Then a man in Native American regalia touched my forehead.

"At that moment, what I will describe as my nonphysical body was thrust down the tunnel, and eventually, it turned into a feeling of total freedom and flying. I was pulled into a bright white light and greeted by my dear grandmother Sarah, who you're named after, and other beings who radiated pure love. My grandmother told me, not in words, but somehow

she told me, that I was much more than I ever thought I was …
that I was home.

"Then I was in another space, void of everything. Yet somehow, I was infinitely powerful. I wanted to stay there forever, but I was hurtled again into another space, where I was introduced to all knowledge. I knew everything there was to know, but as I speak to you now, only a little of that knowledge remains. Then I saw my body on the bed way down below me, and my nonphysical form fell back into it, and I awoke.

"The people I came with seemed relieved; the Native American man was gone. We rested and then went back to Redwood City, where I slept for two days.

"Everything I've ever known and believed had been turned upside down. I had no fear of death. The physical ailments I had before were healed, and I became capable of high-level clustered abstract thinking. I had to get involved in America's space program and the Prometheus Project. Which I did.

"NDEs and medically-induced NDEs can vary greatly, but they all point to one great truth: death of the physical body is not the end. So, I wait for the moment when we can join and embrace unconditional love.

"One more thing: as a second-generation child of the Prometheus Project, you are also a mutant like me."

Sarah started to sob. Johns looked over at her. "What's wrong?"
Tears running down both cheeks, she said, "I understand what you told me about your wife."

* * *

Night fell as they reached the outskirts of Bakersfield, in the San Joaquin Valley. Johns found a place called Red Oaks Ranch, where they could rent a yurt with cash. Cynthia had impressed upon them the need to leave no trail. "Don't use your real names, and avoid credit card purchases," she admonished them. Johns checked them in as Melinda and Frank Peters, brother and sister.

After picking up snacks and drinks, the pair settled in. From the campground, they could easily reach San Jose before noon if they left early. The camp host said it was a four-hour drive.

Tired from driving all day, Johns wanted only to sleep, but his thoughts betrayed him. He knew nothing about his traveling companion, who had ensnared him in intrigue that had nearly gotten him killed within the first twenty-four hours of their acquaintance.

Sarah lay on her bedroll on the other side of the circular tent. Moonlight through the skylight at the top of the tent glinted off her eyes. She wasn't asleep, and Johns decided it was time to find out what was really going on. He sat up on the cot and rested his feet on the wooden plank floor. She swiveled her head toward him. Moments later, she also sat up and met his gaze. She broke the silence first, which was what he preferred.

"What's wrong? Why are you staring at me?"

Johns frowned. "We don't know each other. Yet here we are... in a rather unusual mission."

"What do you want to know?"

"A little context for why someone tried to kill me and Zack. Maybe they're after you, too."

Sarah took a deep breath. "You deserve that."

"So, what gives?"

"I didn't know myself until now. I still don't have all the pieces."

"Tell me what you do know. Maybe I can fill in the blanks."

She ran her hands through her hair. "The flash drive Cynthia gave me was a video of my father telling me about his medically induced near-death experience. He was there at the beginning of the Prometheus Project." She paused, reached down for her canteen, and took a sip of water. Johns did the same. "His name was Simon Ravensbach. He was murdered right in front of me less than a year ago."

"Did they ever figure out who did it and why?"

"It's still an open case, but I suspect that the reason he was murdered has to do with the Prometheus Project."

The scene in the cave flashed in Johns' head. "Christ," he muttered. All the tiredness left him. He stood and walked around the yurt, slapping one hand into the other.

"Isaac, there's something I need to tell you."

Johns' brow furrowed slightly. "What is it?"

She took a deep breath, clearly wrestling with her thoughts before speaking again. "There's something going on with the children of those who've been involved in ... the NDE experiments in the caves. I didn't want to believe it at first. But now, I can't ignore it."

Johns studied her face, the seriousness of her tone piquing his curiosity. "What do you mean?"

"I've been trying to piece it together for a while. But after seeing Cynthia's report on the Prometheus Project and listening to my father earlier... it makes sense. The people running these experiments... they're not just chasing knowledge—they're changing people."

Johns leaned forward slightly, receptive to her opening up in a way she hadn't yet. "What are you saying?"

Her lips pressed into a thin line as if building up the courage to speak. "I'm one of them. One of the children affected by those experiments. And... I have certain abilities. Precognitive ones."

The air between them electrified, as though her words drew a line between the world they knew and something far beyond it. Johns remained quiet, absorbing the weight of her confession. He'd suspected for two days there was more to her than she let on but hearing it directly from her was something else entirely.

Sarah risked a glance at him. "I've known for a while, what they were doing with the experiments, but I refused to accept it."

Johns' gaze didn't waver. "You should have told me."

"I didn't know how," she whispered, her voice thick with vulnerability. "But I'm telling you now."

Across the darkened yurt, unspoken understanding passed between them. Their subtle, imperceptible yet growing connection became, in this shared silence, undeniable.

Johns nodded slowly, his mind racing with the implications of her revelation. But something deeper stirred within him—a realization this journey bound them in ways neither of them anticipated.

"Whatever this means," Johns said, keeping his voice steady, "we'll figure it out. Together."

Sarah exhaled, the tension building inside her easing. For the first time in months, she wasn't carrying the weight of it all alone.

They fell into silence again, but this time it felt different—natural, comfortable. Johns turned his gaze to the stars overhead. The yurt's plasticine ceiling showed the valley's night sky in all its glory. The dynamic had shifted between them. They weren't two strangers on the same path anymore. They were in this together, for better or worse.

Sarah broke the silence. "There's more. Since I was young, I've had precognitive visions about the end to humanity that are more like they belong to someone else, not me—like I'm seeing the future through someone else's eyes. But it's not scary. I've always had a sense there was a solution, though I could never imagine what it could be."

"A familiar apocalyptic motif in today's society."

"Recently, I had a vision that I knew was mine of a man struggling to tell me what I was missing. He was in great agony, but I was sure he had the answer. Then when you showed up with Zack, I immediately recognized that person as you."

A jolt of energy shivered through Johns' whole body. "No wonder you looked at me so strangely. Sorry, I wish I knew the answer. There's something about you I felt right away. I knew you were different... like you were from another species." He smiled self-consciously. "No offense intended."

She laughed. "None taken."

"At first, when Zack proposed the project, I was reluctant, but... because of my interest in the Eleusinian mysteries, I gave in. My reluctance vanished after I looked into the Eye when we were in the cave."

"Can you tell me more of what you saw?"

"Better than that. I'll show you."

Johns dug inside his pack then went to Sarah's cot and sat down. He held the Eye in front of them. "Look at it. You'll see what I mean."

As the moonlight touched the cold stone tablet, she saw her father surrounded by a pure light. The intense aura blew away her ego, and for several seconds she bathed in the incandescence of pure love.

After half a minute, Johns pulled it from her hands and wrapped it in the deerskin.

"Wow, that was powerful."

"Very... what are we going to do with it?"

"That's the big question, isn't it? What the hell are we doing?" Sarah broke into laughter, and Johns joined her.

Once they both settled down, wiping tears from their eyes from laughing so hard, Johns said, "Whatever we do, I feel a sense of urgency about it... a strong sense of urgency."

"Explain what you mean."

"About ten years ago, I was obsessed with Madame Blavatsky. She was a Russian-American mystic and author who co-founded the Theosophical Society in 1875. I read everything I could find about her, interviewed people who wrote books about her, and of course, I learned everything I could about Theosophy. The need to know more was so urgent that at times I stayed up all night."

Sarah laughed. "My senior thesis was about the New Age movement. I know now it coincided with the beginning of the Prometheus Project. And of course, Theosophy turned out to be the foundation of the New Age movement and the counterculture... masters of occult powers, the astral plane, auras, Egyptology, psychedelics, all the good stuff."

"That was the conclusion I came to myself. Belief in the 'one divine source' idea."

She thought of her father as part of the New Age movement. "It just came to me: I think the issue with the Prometheus Project is the method of selecting the initiates. It's a kind of artificial selection by an elite group of people whose purpose we don't understand."

"Controlling the fate of humanity for their own ends, or saving humanity?"

"Let's agree to push on with the same sense of urgency, until the end, whatever that is."

"I'm good with that."

Johns returned to his cot after stuffing the stone votive into his bag beneath. He settled into the three-season sleeping bag provided by the ranch owner. He still couldn't sleep. One more question nagged at him, and he had to ask, or he'd never get any rest. "One more thing?"

Sleepily, Sarah said, "Okay."

Johns chose his words. "How did you get involved in what was obviously a setup?"

"As my father lay dying, he instructed me to contact a dear friend—a general—who convinced me that doing this would illuminate the dark reasons behind my father's murder." Sarah's voice trailed off as the shadows whispered around them. "And of course, I knew the Sedona area quite well."

"You've been there before?"

"My father used to take me there. We'd visit the vortexes. Occasionally, he'd have midnight vigils with others... colleagues, I assumed. I'd sneak out of bed and listen."

"You're not going to say who these men were?" Johns' voice was a blend of curiosity and caution.

"Not now."

The weight of secrecy hung heavy in the air. Johns wondered, but did not ask, if this was the same producer who got him and Zach into this series of extraordinary events.

27

—————

THE DOMINICAN
CLAREMONT, CALIFORNIA

The Dominican friar looked up from the red wax seal bearing the imprint of the Holy See to the young priest standing in front of the wide mahogany desk. "The Holy Father sent this?"

"Y...y...yes, A...Abbot," the young man stammered. He was inexperienced, and his Latin atrocious; he'd bungled the traditional greeting —*Laudetur Jesus Christus*—by saying *lavatur* instead. Now he fidgeted in the monastery's office, nervously kneading his hands into one another, like a schoolboy sent to the principal.

"Wait outside," the Abbot ordered, dismissing the papal emissary with a perfunctory wave.

"Dominus vobiscum et cum spiritu tuo," the priest said, his accent pitiful, and left.

The Abbot waited until the room was empty then read the address on the outside of the parchment: *To be delivered personally into the hands of Abbot Friar Augustus, Dominican Monastery, Claremont, California.* Twenty years prior, the Vatican had established the priory in what was once a Jewish synagogue in the small university town of Claremont.

He opened the message, careful to preserve the wax seal intact. The text would appear meaningless to anyone unfamiliar with the code, yet the message would self-destruct instantly if the Papal seal were broken. The words sent a chill down his spine. *Augustus, old friend, time is against us. You must find the Eye and destroy it as soon as you can.* The message had been signed with the Holy Father's name, the handwriting recognizable.

He laid the paper on the desk and gazed out the room's only window onto a garden where two members of the small order tended to the flowers. The Pope's decision to send a messenger, especially one as untried and untested as this youth, indicated the Vatican's urgent desire that the votive relief not fall into the wrong hands.

Friar Augustus suppressed a shudder. So close to fulfillment. The first part was already in his possession. He glanced at the painting on the wall behind him. Raphael's *The Resurrection of Christ* dominated the otherwise austere room. Hidden behind the picture lay the priory's safe, containing the original Dead Sea Scroll that described Christ's near-death experience in the desert.

If I don't find the Eye, humankind will perish... and God's creation will be undone, he thought.

Rising from the old desk, he flexed his fingers. Outside, the monastery's bell tolled eight. The sun had risen above the walls, and those brothers not already in the dining room shuffled along the brick walkways to the chapel for prayers before breaking their evening fast. He stretched his back, feeling the weight of the responsibility to find the Eye. Not a burden, but a calling from an early age.

Friar Augustus had been born William "Bill" Gallagher into a middle-class Irish Catholic family in a small farm village on Ireland's west coast. At the age of four, he suffered a fall down a flight of stairs, resulting in a broken arm and a severe head wound. The subsequent infection nearly claimed his life; at one point, his parents feared he had passed away. Miraculously, he stirred, rolled over, and reassured his mother, "I'm okay, Mam."

For the next two years, every night, apparitions of deceased members of his family appeared to Bill. He hid under his bed until one of his parents came into his room to comfort him. Eventually, one of the fathers at their local parish recommended an exorcism. The belief was that the devil had somehow joined with Bill during the height of his delirious state caused by the infection. The exorcism was traumatic for the whole family, and rumors of devilry haunted the Gallaghers for years afterward.

At the age of seven, William's family emigrated to Los Angeles. His extraordinary ordeal had become a distant memory except for an inexplicable result. From birth, he had been an ordinary child with only a passing interest in things around him. After his near-death experience, his intellect blossomed. Teachers placed him in advanced science and math programs; eventually, he enrolled early at Caltech University in Pasadena, California—a prestigious institution known for its contributions to modern science with a rigorous focus on pure and applied sciences. William seamlessly integrated into this environment.

Before his graduation, Northrop Grumman recruited him to work on highly classified defense projects. Following a corporate acquisition by Lockheed Martin two years later, a fellow Irishman, Sam Hill, invited him to join the secretive Prometheus Project. William's initiation was the third to take place in a cave near Sedona, Arizona, and proceeded without incident, yet he emerged visibly shaken, haunted by memories of his near-death experience as a child and convinced of a demonic presence behind the ordeal.

Sam Hill and Gallagher stayed in touch, meeting clandestinely, often debating the ethics of the artificial procedure for selecting candidates. During one of these meetings, Hill showed Gallagher the origin paper written by Gunderson. Gallagher was horrified.

Unknown to the others of the Prometheus Project, Gallagher was determined to halt the barbaric practice. He left the aerospace industry and disappeared for ten years, resurfacing in Rome as the Dominican Friar Augustus. His former connections within the aerospace industry eventually led to an invitation to the Vatican Observatory, where he developed a friendship with the Vatican's premier astronomer, Cardinal Giovanni Sandri. Eventually, Augustus confided in him about the Prometheus Project, seeking assistance to end it.

In response, the Vatican devised a covert plan to support Augustus's efforts, concluding that public knowledge of Jesus having a pedestrian, drug-induced hallucination during his fast in the wilderness instead of the literal battle against Satan's temptation as written by Matthew and Luke could tear down the Church. Imagine the chaos if every person could directly receive the same enlightenment as the Son of God. To facilitate his mission, the Church appointed Augustus as the Abbot of a small monastery in Claremont, California. The ultimate goal was to acquire and destroy the critical artifacts of the project—the Scroll and the Eye. Should any off-the-record work be necessary, the Vatican had operatives skilled in resolving such matters.

Now Friar Augustus, fair-haired and gray-eyed, was in his early forties, tall and trim, with the ruddy features of an Irish farmer. He wore a simple white robe and black sandals, a far cry from his stifling work clothes in aerospace, which felt like a lifetime ago.

He settled into the plain Shaker chair. The monastery was quiet, the other monks in the chapel attending Vespers. Outside a full moon rose above the walls. *A fall harvest moon,* he thought idly. *Hopefully, we will harvest the fruits of our search for the Eye.*

He turned to face the Raphael painting. Over the years, he had often contemplated what he considered to be the master's artistic triumph. The vibrancy of Christ's awakening from death gave him great personal solace. Tonight, Augustus needed that comfort. He dialed a number on his phone.

"Sam Hill," a mellifluous voice answered.

Augustus inquired, "How's our young friend doing?"

"Snyder's dropped off the grid."

Augustus's jaw dropped. "You have no idea where?"

"Behind you," Snyder answered.

28

—————

JANUS SNYDER'S NEXT MOVE
CLAREMONT, CALIFORNIA

Friar Augustus spun around, his heart rate accelerating, to find Janus Snyder materializing from the office's shadows. He quickly ended the call to Sam Hill and scrutinized the young man before him. Snyder's posture was rigid, shoulders drawn back, veins in his neck visibly pulsing—a testament to his barely contained intensity. Despite being unarmed, the deadly potential of Snyder's hands and feet was not lost on Friar Augustus, who knew the importance of maintaining an unwavering facade before the former soldier. His voice, heavy with authority and the echoes of untold stories, was like a controlled tempest. "I explicitly warned you—never to contact me directly."

Snyder's response cut sharply through the heavy atmosphere. "Well, circumstances have shifted."

"So, I've gathered," Friar Augustus retorted, his tone dripping with skepticism as dense as the tension suffusing the room.

Snyder leaned in closer, his face etched with urgency, as if every second was precious. "The operation was compromised. It felt like the contact was pursuing his own objectives."

Recalling a previous entanglement where Snyder had proven his worth, Friar Augustus's tone softened, if only marginally. "You were right before—when you secured the scroll and resolved the situation with Sarah's father."

"What's our next move?"

"We bide our time. But be prepared; I'll need you in the coming days. Can I count on you?" Friar Augustus's tone filled the room with silent anticipation.

Snyder's frustration was written on his face, his demand for transparency unmistakable. "What's really going on here? I'm done with all this secrecy."

"Our goal remains unchanged." Friar Augustus met Snyder's gaze with unwavering intensity. The storm of unspoken plans and steely resolve swirled between them, hinting at the brewing conflict that lay ahead.

29

DESERT SOLITAIRE
MOJAVE DESERT

Zack watched the last rays of the sun fade against the San Bernardino Mountains. The temperature dropped precipitously with the sun, so he hustled inside the rustic cabin. He built a fire in the small cast iron stove, which quickly banished the Mojave Desert's night cold. Solar panels on the roof provided enough light for the twin LED bulbs hanging above the crude desk beneath the cabin's only window. Outside, coyotes howled at the rising gibbous moon that cast a baleful glare on the yuccas and cacti ringing the natural spring where he drew water.

Plugging his laptop into the cabin's only outlet, he launched his editing software, copied the footage to his hard drive, and settled down to review what he shot in the cave. The hospital equipment was perplexing, but the cave walls were something out of an Indiana Jones movie. The symbols painted on the rock echoed ancient Egyptian hieroglyphs, but there were also Greek letters, which he recalled from his pledge days at Princeton. He also thought some of the figures might be Celtic Runes.

Zack shook his head at the images. "This shit is all over the place. What the hell did I get mixed up in?" He peered closely at a symbol displayed prominently to the left of the gurney. He enlarged the picture, using one of the edit system tools to clean up the image. "I'll be damned," he said, smiling as he recognized the symbol. "The Owl of Minerva, Roman goddess of wisdom. Isaac will know about that."

The coyote calls stopped.

Zack looked up from the computer screen and stared into the night. He saw nothing toward the pond. His father's shotgun nestled in a rack behind the stove. He got up but at the same time the door to the shack burst inward, revealing the silhouette of a man. Zack lunged for the shotgun. Something hard hit him in the right side of his chest and spun him around. A thousand volts shot through his body, and he collapsed on the floor.

* * *

Sound returned first, and then sight. Zack was tied to the chair. The man was scrolling through his computer. He glanced at Zack. A scar ran down his right cheek and disappeared into his shirt collar. He had sandy, thinning hair and wore rose-tinted sunglasses. Zack opened his mouth, but no words came out.

The intruder stood up from the computer. "Don't try to talk yet; the electroshock bullet takes a few minutes to wear off. Technically, it's called a piezoelectric incapacitation projectile. It isn't lethal, but it packs quite a punch."

The man walked around the shack, nodding approvingly at the layout. "This is a great place you have here. Well off the beaten track. Would never have found you if you hadn't made that phone call. We were able to pinpoint your location."

Zack found his voice. "Who's we?"

"Friends ... friends of God, you might say." He jerked a thumb at the computer. "We don't like the idea of that kinda stuff getting out to the masses, making them question their beliefs."

Zack paled. "What do you want with me?"

"Answer a few questions, and you're free."

Zack's face registered fear.

"Is this your only copy?"

Zack thought of the hard drive he'd given Isaac. "It's still on the SD card in my camera."

The man smashed the computer and removed the hard drive. Then he ejected the SD card from the camera. "Swell. Now about your friends."

"My friends?"

"Yeah. The ones who dropped you off here ... Sarah and Isaac."

Zack opened his mouth to object, but the man waved a beefy hand at him. "Don't deny it. There're car tracks leading here and your footprints in the dirt. No other vehicles around. Where'd they go?"

Zack shook his head. "I hitchhiked in."

The man sighed. "And we were doing so well." He went over to the stove and opened the door with a thick pad put there for that purpose. He pulled out a hot poker Zack used to stoke the fire. The man must have put it in the stove while he was out cold. He brought the red-hot tip over and held it close to Zack's right eye. The heat seared the soft skin of his eyelids. "Now Zack, I don't want to be overly dramatic, but you can see where this is going to go if you don't cooperate."

Zack nodded. He wasn't a hero. "Okay. They're on their way to San Jose to meet some guy named Gunderson. I don't know where. Honest."

The man smiled and set the poker on the floor. It burned the wood, and pine smoke drifted into the air. "I believe you. What does this Gunderson do?"

"He's a thought leader of some kind. Isaac Johns knows him."

"Nice of you to be so cooperative."

The man went to the stove. "These things are dangerous. You never know when they might fall over." He kicked the side. The door flew open and hot coals spilled out onto the wooden planks. Smoke rose into the cabin.

The man turned at the door. "If you stay in the chair, chances are the smoke will kill you before the flames burn you alive." He laughed ghoulishly. "Just so you know before you die, my name is Francis Xavier Mellon." He left, slamming the door closed.

Zack stared at the smoke thickening the air. Flames spread across the flooring to the walls. The dry wood caught fire quickly.

He cursed Francis Xavier Mellon, "May you die in hell."

30

GUNDERSON

SAN JOAQUIN VALLEY, CALIFORNIA

Sarah and Johns rose before the sun cleared the tips of the Sierra Nevada Mountains. They quickly stowed their gear in Cynthia's Range Rover, and then Sarah slid behind the wheel. The tension and excitement of what lay ahead hung as thickly in the air as the early morning fog.

Skirting Bakersfield to the east, the pair stopped briefly at the Old Southern Pacific Railroad Station for sandwiches and coffee before hitting California State Highway 69 north to Fresno. Cynthia had warned them to stay off the interstate in the valley, which was monitored with traffic cams. At Fresno, they'd turn west, crossing I-5 to Hollister before turning north again to San Jose. It was a simple plan, designed to keep them off the grid as much as possible, though it would take longer than driving straight up the interstate.

They traveled in silence, the fog inhibiting them as much as Cynthia's warning to keep as low a profile as possible. Outside Delano the sun broke through the fog. The central valley's agricultural vista spread before them.

Johns took in the vastness of the farms surrounding them. "I've never been here before. I had no idea it was so big."

"You should see it in the summer," Sarah said. "It's so green it looks like an ocean."

Johns checked his phone's map app. "By my calculation, we should arrive at Gunderson's place in less than four hours."

Sarah looked over at Johns with a frown.

"What's wrong?" he asked.

"You never told me why you felt compelled to contact Gunderson even before Cynthia told us about his role in the Prometheus Project."

"He's an odd character. We met a few times at conferences. He's an incredible tech innovator, a Renaissance man who was promoting his book, *The Immortality Solution,* when we first met. We discussed some of his unorthodox ideas."

"Which were?"

"In the early twenty-first century, Gunderson wrote a peculiar book arguing that the sacraments which shaped Western civilization were unknown, mind-altering drugs used by initiates who were brought to the brink of death in Eleusis, Greece."

"Where that relic you call 'the Eye' originated."

"Right... at least that's what the current evidence suggests."

"There must be more?"

Johns' eyebrow arched. "I'm surprised you asked that question. You heard what Cynthia said about his role in the Prometheus Project."

"I get his connection to it. But why did you choose to contact him before you knew about his connection to the project?"

"From our conversations at conferences, I got the impression he was making himself available to be contacted if anyone uncovered what those drugs might have been or even caught a whiff of something like the Prometheus Project."

"So, who is he when he isn't writing books about the history of Western civilization?"

"He runs a modest think tank called 'Spiritual Transformations for a Sustainable Worldview'... At the time, he had a lovely wife who managed his activities ... He is deeply involved in the study of meditation and maintains a close connection with the Dalai Lama."

"So, he's well-known."

"Yes and no." Johns laughed at her puzzled expression. "People who attend these types of conferences know him in the way people communicated before the Internet. On the other hand, he has nearly zero web presence."

"That's probably because of his prominent role in the Prometheus Project. I'm quite excited to meet him; he must know my contacts."

Sarah's phone buzzed. She tapped the connect button on the cart's steering wheel. Cynthia's alto voice came over the Rover's speaker system. "Good morning. I hope the two of you have been keeping a low profile so far." She hurried on before either Sarah or Johns could reply, "Change of plans. You're to meet Gunderson in the office of Superintendent Beth Kearny at Pinnacles National Park." The call went dead.

Johns brought up the Google Maps app on his phone, punched in the new address, and whistled appreciatively. "That'll shave an hour off our travel time." After a pause, he said, "There's one more thing. When I met Gunderson, I had a strong feeling we were already connected in some way I don't understand."

31

GUNDERSON

PINNACLES NATIONAL PARK

At Pinnacles National Park's west entrance, Isaac Johns got out of the Range Rover and stretched his legs. Overhead, a California Condor circled. He watched the endangered bird soar for a hundred yards then grabbed a park brochure. Back in the car, he opened it up and read to Sarah. "Geologically, the Talus Caves at the park were primarily formed by volcanic activity over twenty-three million years ago. The movement of the Pacific Plate over volcanic fields caused eruptions and flowing lava, which, upon cooling, created the rock pinnacle formations characteristic of the park. Particularly on the less-developed western side, the park contains a complex network of talus caves formed by boulders falling into narrow canyons, creating cavernous passageways and chambers that are still being explored today."

"It makes sense, doesn't it?" Sarah mused. "Those caves would be the closest to Silicon Valley when the project was getting going during the sixties and seventies counterculture movement."

Inside the visitor center, Sarah and Johns walked up to the reception desk. An exuberant female ranger immediately greeted them with an inviting smile. "You must be Sarah and Isaac. The Superintendent's office is around the corner; just go in."

The door opened noiselessly. An overhead light lit the room. The spartan office held a simple desk with two chairs in front. A file cabinet beside the desk was the only other furniture. Perched on the edge of the desk sat Gerald Gunderson.

The man did not look like he had aged since he and Johns last met.

Upon seeing the pair, Gunderson's thin lips parted in a big smile, and in an age-defying move, he jumped off the desk to greet them. "Good to see you again, Dr. Johns, and to finally meet you, Sarah. I knew your father." Pointing to Johns' backpack, he inquired, "The stone votive is in there?" His gaze narrowed, and the kindly fatherly look changed to a more demanding glare. He stood from the desk and held out his hand. "Let me see it."

Johns backed away from the look of avarice on the older man's face.

Sarah stepped between them. "Why should we show it to you?"

The menacing stare evaporated, and a kindly look covered Gunderson's pale Scandinavian complexion. He returned to his seat on the desk. "Please let me see it; it's been a while."

Johns eyed him skeptically but took off his backpack and pulled out the carefully wrapped stone.

He handed the package to Gunderson. The old man's powerful fingers peeled back the deer hide. The image of Athena stared up at him. He let out a long slow breath, ending in a grateful sigh. His eyes never left the stone, transfixed by its presence.

"Thank you for saving it." His lips pursed as he studied Johns for a moment. "The effect it has—quite something, isn't it?"

"Yes, I've entered an unusual state of mind a couple of times," Johns admitted.

Gunderson chuckled. "Of course you would. Do you remember the second time we met at the conference in New Orleans? We went for a walk together in a nearby cemetery."

Thinking back to the conference, Johns shook his head. "Are you sure we did?"

"I thought that might be the case, that you wouldn't remember."

"Remember what?" Johns asked, bewildered by the strange turn in the conversation.

"What happened during that walk made clear to me you were the right person."

Johns shook his head helplessly. He turned toward Sarah. "Do you know what he's talking about?"

"I'm as in the dark as you. What's this about, sir?"

"Yeah," Johns echoed. "The right person for what?"

"For what lies ahead. We'll discuss that soon enough. For now, we are good."

Johns changed the subject. "The Eye is supposedly in the Athens National Archaeological Museum."

"Yes. The one in their collection is authentic. Three were made that we know of. Where the third one is, or if there are any others, nobody knows." He handed the Eye back to Johns. The skin around his eyes crinkled with laughter. "Welcome to the game. Let's head out to the original cave. I'll explain everything as we go."

Gunderson slung a large backpack over his shoulder with the ease of a man half his age and led them to the back door of the office. Waiting outside was a large Black man in blue battle fatigues, whom Gunderson introduced with a gesture. "This is Beast."

The man laughed in a deep, strong voice. "From the X-Men. We are the mutants, aren't we?"

"Beast is on loan from the NSA," Gunderson explained. "He'll watch our backs as we venture into the cave."

Beast bowed his head. "Let us pray."

His voice became a low, guttural hum, but Johns recognized the words—a traditional invocation to Athena. He closed his eyes and repeated the prayer. Beside him, Sarah instinctively joined.

When the humming ceased, Sarah rocked back on her heels. She feared to open her eyes lest the surreal feeling coursing through her vanished. Indeed, she had never felt so profoundly connected to everything, as if she were destined to play a crucial role in a story unfolding for centuries. "What just happened?" she whispered, bewildered. She opened her eyes. Beast had vanished. Johns and Gunderson were talking.

When the humming ended, Johns' heart hammered madly. Beast's invocation triggered an epiphany. He turned to Gunderson. "Of course! The prayer explains all the stories about how the awakening rituals from Eleusis persisted through the centuries after Christ's death, especially among the Gnostic Christians."

Gunderson nodded, a look of fatherly pride illuminating his face. He motioned to Sarah to join them, his gaze intent. "Cynthia mentioned you know your father played a pivotal role in this grand experiment we call the Prometheus Project. Have you begun to understand your part in it?"

Sarah nodded. Her feeling of oneness continued, and she felt an undeniable connection to Gunderson, as if their destinies were intertwined.

Sensing her reaction, he continued, "Your purpose is to save the future of humanity. That's your mission, isn't it?"

Sarah found her voice. "Yes."

"Simon always said you were the brightest of our second-generation children, and I believe he's right." Gunderson led the pair outside to the parking lot.

"The Eleusinian ritual had a purpose, I presume?" Johns asked as they headed toward a Jeep parked on the far side of the lot.

"Of course, reminding us we're not in control," Gunderson replied. His dark blue eyes scanned the horizon as if expecting unwelcome company.

"Why do we need someone watching our backs?"

"Because there's a lot at stake in what we're involved in, and not everyone wants us to succeed." Gunderson stowed his pack in the back of the jeep. He motioned to Johns to hold onto the Eye. "Keep it safe. Where we're going, the trail is treacherous."

Gunderson took off at a speed that transgressed the speed limit. Sarah and Johns buckled their seat belts and held on.

From the other end of the lot, a man watched them depart. He smiled. *The filmmakers' information was correct.* He started his pickup and eased after Gunderson and the other two. The Dominican's orders had been clear: "Francis, your first part of the mission is to find out where they're going. Then take the Eye and destroy the markings on the wall."

"Yes, Father," he had answered solemnly.

Francis Xavier Mellon was a devoutly pious man. The Saint Christopher's medal he wore represented only one of the many patron saints he called upon to aid his part in the cause. He stayed well behind his quarry, not wishing to tip them off that their time had come. He sensed the dark foreboding hanging in the air; his mission must succeed if the Church was to maintain control of God's kingdom on Earth. *"Deus ambulabit mecum et benedicat mihi,"* he whispered, and then kissed the medal. *May God Walk with me and bless me.* He pushed the medal back inside his shirt. A plan to grab the eye unfolded in his mind.

32

MAJOR MARTIN DAVIDSON

CHIMERA LAB, 29 PALMS MARINE BASE, CALIFORNIA

Major Martin Davidson, a tall and fit Corpsman in his early thirties, approached his work area in a white lab coat with his rank insignia on the shoulders over blue surgical scrubs, a surgical cap securing his dark hair from inadvertent escape. He held one gray eye to the oval retinal scanner beside the metal door leading to the Regenerative Bio-Electrical Lab. A soft whine was followed by a click, and the door swung open.

Behind him, Lance Corporal Adrian Henderson said, "Feels like coming home, sir." He smiled, showing perfect white teeth in an olive-colored face. His dark eyes gleamed unnaturally bright in the corridor's dimmed lighting. A thin red line across his forehead crinkled. "Why am I here?"

"You started your return to normal inside."

The corporal laughed. "Don't I know it. When I arrived, I thought you were just going to use me as a guinea pig then forget about me like everybody else."

Davidson frowned. "Wouldn't do that. I'm not that kind of person."

The two men bumped fists and entered the lab.

The spacious room was divided into two parts. The first half held desks and numerous computer terminals. The second was a state-of-the-art cell research lab. One side was dominated by a flow cytometer, used for counting and sorting cells as well as for biomarker detection, and centrifuges that isolated and purified cells and subcellular organelles. Against the other wall sat an argon-ion laser, which fluorescently labeled cells, and detectors to measure the light emitted, allowing for analysis of electrical and chemical characteristics of cells. Two large confocal microscopes captured detailed images of structures within cells in both live and fixed samples. Scattered on lab benches throughout the room, incubators and CO_2 chambers cultivated and maintained cell cultures under controlled temperature, humidity, and gas concentration for fundamental tissue culture work.

Davidson led the lance corporal down a narrow hallway to a second laboratory with four large isolation chambers. A phantasmagorical creature occupied one of the chambers. It had an appendage reminiscent of a bird of prey, six other appendages resembling the arms of an octopus, and still others that looked like pincers belonging to a praying mantis. It appeared to be growing a central sensor.

Corporal Henderson's jaw dropped. "What the hell, Doc?"

Davidson grinned. "She's a chimera."

"Like in Greek mythology?"

"Yes. Only instead of breathing fire, Elsie is a product of combining and programming tissue from a flatworm, an octopus, and a praying mantis, among other species. She's immortal and reproduces by binary fission, not sexually. Two more of these prototypes are already engaged in simulated battle situations at another lab on the base."

Henderson nodded knowingly at the creatures. "You did something similar to me."

"Every human body has the capability of regenerating fingers when it is very young. For you, we were able to bring online, through bioelectrical programming, the collective intelligence of the cells that already know how to regenerate hands."

Henderson shook his head. "At the time I thought you were manipulating my genome."

"Not at all. What we're doing is highly classified, so I couldn't tell you the details "

"Still, I'm grateful, sir, but Christ, that's a shock. I..." he flexed his fingers. "I'm grateful."

"I know you are. That's why I asked you to be transferred to this facility under my command." Davidson beckoned Henderson to an office at the back of the lab, and he followed. "You handled the transition from disabled to totally healed better than anyone else who has come into this facility. I think you can help us with a new line of self-healing I want to try."

Henderson's luminous eyes narrowed. "Anything you say, sir. Without you, I'd be nothing more than a blind, homeless vet without any hands." He curled his fingers. The knuckles popped, and he laughed quietly.

"You underrate yourself."

Lance Corporal Henderson had been on patrol in Helmand Province with one day left on his tour when the IED exploded in front of him. His hands were shredded and both eyes were destroyed by tiny slivers of steel. Shipped stateside, he'd languished at Walter Reed in Washington, DC, for two months until he received a notice to report to the Marine Air Corps Air Ground Combat Center near 29 Palms, California. The irony of a blind, handless Marine reporting to a combat group was not lost on him, and he let his anger show when Major Davidson met him in the lab for the first time two years ago.

"I'm Major Martin Davidson, Corporal. We're going to fix you up," the Marine Doctor had said assuredly.

"Grow me new eyes and hands?" Henderson replied bitterly. "Fat chance."

"We're going to do exactly that. You'll be your old self in less than a year. You have my word on it."

Henderson felt awe at the calm assurance of the doctor's promise. "No fooling, sir?" he said, with something like hope for the first time since the IED exploded.

"Guaranteed."

Henderson laughed. "It sounds all so easy now, looking back on it. Still, I wouldn't be here if it weren't for you. Thanks."

Davidson smiled. "I provided the technology. You did all the hard work."

Henderson nodded. "I still can't believe you taught my cells to regenerate."

Davidson laughed. "We didn't really teach them anything. My team simply reminded the cells what they already knew how to do."

Davidson stopped, and his tone became serious. "I want you to meet someone, Adrian. We're heading up a unique program trying to unlock latent human capabilities. We think you're the man who can help us."

"Who am I meeting?"

Davidson opened the door to his office and ushered Henderson inside. A tall man in civilian clothes with cropped graying hair, a tanned face, and a hard smile rose from the room's only chair behind a small desk with a computer interface on it.

"Corporal, I want you to meet General Deke Davidson, my father."

Henderson came immediately to attention. His hand shot up in a salute. The general returned it crisply.

"At ease, Marine."

Henderson stood with his legs apart and his hands clasped behind his back. The general nodded approvingly.

"Did my son tell you what this is all about?"

"Only that you need my help, sir."

"Good. Sit down and wait here. My son and I are going out for a walk."

Major Davidson and the general left the office. They threaded through the lab out into the corridor. Martin opened his mouth, but the general waved him to silence. "Not here, son." He indicated the cameras in the corridor. He led the doctor outside.

The air was sere, and the sky a harsh blue. In the distance, a low range of mountains thrust out of the desert. The base was devoid of any vegetation except for protected Joshua trees encircling the large command compound on the huge 29 Palms Marine Base. The foothills supported a variety of cacti and yuccas.

Out of nowhere, two large explosions made the ground tremble underfoot. The two men jumped, and then laughed in a way unique to father and son.

"By the way, your stepmom sends her blessings, as usual."

"You and Cynthia should have stayed together."

"In our own way, we do, of course."

When they were well away from the building, the general looked sternly at his son. "Who the hell is that guy?"

"Lance Corporal Adrian Henderson. He worked closely with a battalion's intelligence officer while doing three tours in Afghanistan. Speaks Farsi, Pashto, and Arabic. Bronze and silver stars before being sent home blind and crippled."

The general's eyes widened. "Shit. He looks perfectly normal."

"Thanks to technology developed at my lab and his body's exceptional ability to respond to our bioelectric programming."

"And just why the hell is he here?"

"He's volunteered to be the test subject in the next step of the Prometheus Project."

"Bullshit. I'm the test subject."

"With all due respect, sir, that's a very bad idea."

The general glared at his son, though with no animosity. His brilliant son had developed the technology for a prolonged NDE that would keep people dead for more than fifteen minutes before reviving them. "Explain why I shouldn't have you busted to private and cleaning latrines for hogging all the fun?" He grinned, taking the sting out of his words.

"The next step in the program is more than experimental. It's never been done before."

"I have no fear of death. I've been dead before, as you know."

"Not this long, and not without the Eye and the chants to make sure you're able to return from the nonphysical realm. I want to make sure a prolonged NDE won't kill the initiate outright."

Major General Davidson's forehead furrowed with concern.

"Please, Dad, for Prometheus to achieve its goal, we need you alive to make sure everything goes correctly during the launch."

The general threw his hands up. "Okay, I accept your need to test the hypothesis. When are you going to start the procedure?"

"This morning. My techs are prepping him now."

The general shook his head ruefully. "You knew I'd give in."

"I'd have sedated you if you refused to accept my terms."

The general smiled. "I bet you would have. Can I participate?"

"Wouldn't have it any other way."

33

THE PILGRIMAGE

PINNACLES NATIONAL PARK, CALIFORNIA

Sarah and Johns marveled at the stunning pinnacle spires reaching for the heavens. The brightly colored rock sparkled under the mid-morning sun's rays. Suddenly, Gunderson veered off the main road, throwing his passengers into the Jeep's canvas side. He drove several hundred yards along a narrow hiking trail before stopping beside a circle of boulders.

"Isn't this illegal?" Sarah asked.

"It's the superintendent's personal vehicle," Gunderson replied with a wink.

The trio clambered out and walked to the back. Noticing Gunderson's large, heavy backpack, Sarah offered, "Let me carry that for you."

Gunderson laughed. "I may look like an old man, but because of my medical NDE, I have what might be called superhuman strength." He effortlessly flipped the backpack over his shoulders and took off up the trail, which angled sharply upward.

They had gone a quarter mile when they reached a small crack in the jumbled talus boulders. Pointing, Gunderson said, "We need to squeeze through."

Remembering his exhaustion upon reaching the cave in Arizona, Johns groaned and mumbled, "I could use some of that superhuman strength."

Gunderson grinned. "I also have exceptional hearing. Perhaps you will soon as well."

They took off their packs and crab-walked through the corridor. In the center, it narrowed, the rock walls squeezing Johns' chest and shoulder blades. He gritted his teeth and forced his way through.

As they reached the other side, the corridor opened onto a grassy knoll ringed by more stacked talus boulders. Gunderson paused for a moment. "Dr. Johns, I expect you remember that in the descriptions of the Greek luminaries traveling to Eleusis, they were put into a state of exhaustion. Originally, we assumed this would have to happen as well, which is why the journeys to the cave are so physically difficult."

"Of course. A typical requirement for all successful pilgrimages."

Gunderson turned to Sarah. "Let me ask you, what do you feel right now?"

"Uneasy, but I'm not sure why." She shivered and rubbed her arms. "It's sort of like we're being watched, like knives are pointed at me."

Gunderson smiled at Johns. "What about you?"

"I figured my fear of the unknown was creeping up. It's quite like excitement, isn't it?"

"Well, we are being watched." Gunderson flicked his hand as if swatting away a fly.

Johns realized something important. "Those somebodies who want us not to succeed ... they've already sent someone," he said with a slight chuckle. "Where's Beast?"

"He's already at the cave. Now, it's time to crawl."

Gunderson got down on his hands and knees and began crawling through a tunnel that was just large enough they didn't have to remove their packs.

The way was rocky, and Johns wished he had brought gloves and knee pads. By the time they exited the tunnel, he was tired, thirsty, and his hands were bruised. Sarah looked equally disheveled. Remarkably, Gunderson didn't appear the least bit stressed.

"We're almost there," he said. "Just around this grouping of rocks." He laughed and disappeared around the bend.

34

FRANCIS XAVIER MELLON
PINNACLES NATIONAL PARK

Francis Mellon watched the trio disappear down the trail. The large man in the military uniform was nowhere in sight. *Curious,* he thought. So, Mellon parked his vehicle where Gunderson turned onto the trail then ran at top speed, easily matching the progress of the Jeep. He waited a minute then followed them through the narrow crevice, his steps silent.

The Dominican wanted the Eye, and from what Zack Helm had told him, Johns carried it with him, never letting it out of his sight. Getting it would be a breeze, Mellon thought. Not even Gunderson was likely to match his combat skills. And none of them had the advantage of his years of intense special ops training.

He exited the crevice onto a grassy opening surrounded by talus boulders as big as a car. His quarry had vanished. Mellon's forehead furrowed as he scanned the surrounding cliff faces. No trails led upward. Cursing under his breath, he thought, *I'll ambush them and get the Eye when they return.*

Mellon grinned. Easy peasy. He retraced his steps, confidence oozing from every pore. *With the blessing of the Holy Spirit, this is going to be fun.*

35

─────

THE TALUS CAVE

PINNACLES NATIONAL PARK

Gunderson pushed along the narrow ledge with the speed of someone much younger. "Not much farther," he exhorted over his shoulder before disappearing into another narrow crevice.

Exhausted, Sarah turned behind to relay the message. Johns was nowhere to be seen. She hurried forward through the narrow passage. Several minutes passed before the passageway opened onto a box canyon. Sheer sides towered a hundred feet above them. "Gerald," she gasped. "Isaac isn't with us. He was right behind me."

Gunderson frowned. He turned to retrace his steps when the scrape of boot on rock cut through the still air. Johns emerged from the narrow crevice. "I'm here," he said, his voice ragged. "Took me a while."

"Glad you could join us," Gunderson said drolly. He whistled twice—a long and a short. The call was answered with three short bursts.

Beast emerged from a narrow cave mouth hidden by a stand of what the locals called shrubby butterweed.

"What's going on?" Sarah demanded.

"The truth is never simple. Right now, I need to talk to Beast in private for a few moments."

The two men walked to the other side of the elongated narrow clearing.

In low tones, Gunderson said, "We're being tracked."

"Correct, but he got lost and is now waiting for you to retrace your steps. I believe he will do whatever it takes to get a hold of the Eye."

"Can you neutralize him?"

"He is skilled, but I do not sense he is an initiate like us."

"Find out who he's working for, what they know about our plans, and then do whatever you need to do."

They walked back to Sarah and Johns. Beast pulled out three bottles of water and a pill container, handing them to Johns. "When you're done in the cave, take these. They're fifty times more potent than the speed given to our military personnel ever since World War II."

With a wave and a smile, Beast, with the ease of a bighorn sheep, bounded up a pile of boulders that rose like steps to the canyon's rim and disappeared.

"Cave?" Johns said, bewildered. He was exhausted and thirsty. He wanted the pills Beast had given them now, but Gunderson confiscated both.

Pushing aside the rabbit grass, Gunderson gestured to a narrow opening. "Let's go in."

Inside the cave, as in the one in Sedona, a single beam of light pierced a crack above, illuminating the darkness. Gunderson quickly set up battery-powered lights, and when he flicked the switch, the cave transformed, basking in the glow of a miniature sun.

Though the cave appeared empty, the walls were alive with intricate symbols and numbers, mirroring those in the Sedona cave. Gunderson's voice resonated with urgency. "What you're looking for are any chants hidden among these markings. I can't decipher them, but I believe you can."

Johns pulled out his laptop and handed his backpack, containing the Eye, to Sarah. As he explored, Sarah and Gunderson watched, anticipation hanging in the air. Johns moved with purpose, his eyes darting between the cave walls and the images from Sedona.

Suddenly, he stopped in front of a series of symbols, his expression shifting from concentration to disbelief. "These weren't in the other cave," he stated, his voice low.

Gunderson didn't reply but sat on the large rock positioned where he and Sarah could observe Johns' work.

Johns traced the symbols with his fingers, photographing them one by one. The more he studied them, the more an overwhelming significance radiated from the markings. But something was off; the symbols seemed misaligned, as if their true meaning was just out of reach.

Stepping back, he squatted down, gazing upward at the images. Clarity emerged from the haze, and then it struck him—he was resonating with the minds of the Prometheus Project founders who painted these symbols long ago.

As he scanned the cave, his gaze landed on a niche against the far wall, revealing a stone pallet inches off the ground. He lay down on the dusty rock, tilting his head to read the symbols from bottom to top. His breath caught in his throat, and time itself dissolved as Sarah and Gunderson faded into the background.

With each deep breath, a softness enveloped his vision, allowing him to see beyond the artwork. Light pulsed from the edges of each symbol, drawing inward until the images glowed with an inner fire. Tears streamed down his face as an overwhelming magnitude of understanding flooded his mind. Sobs echoed in the small space, each one a release of the emotions swelling inside him.

"Isaac!" Sarah's voice broke through the haze as she rushed to his side, shaking him gently.

His eyes locked onto hers before shifting to Gunderson, who stood anxiously nearby. Taking a deep breath to steady the tempest of knowledge surging within him, Johns declared, "I know what the symbols are... what the chant is."

Johns stood as if pulled upward by an unseen force and walked to the wall of symbols. Gunderson and Sarah rushed over, their eyes wide with anticipation. Holding out his phone, Johns pointed the cursor at a series of symbols. "Look! Each symbol represents a vowel in five languages, starting with Greek and ending with English. It's a, e, i, o, u—the fundamental sounds of all languages. Many believe this was the dawn of consciousness for our species!"

"What does it sound like?" Sarah asked, her excitement infectious.

In deep, guttural tones, Johns chanted the sounds over and over, the vibrations resonating in the cave's walls.

"That's it! I remember now," Gunderson said, his voice brimming with energy. "Let's chant together!"

Their voices united, reverberating through the cave with newfound power.

Somewhat breathless, Sarah pulled the Eye from the backpack.

"One more time, looking at the Eye," Gunderson suggested, his enthusiasm shared by all. As they chanted again, the echoes intensified, enveloping them in a wave of energy.

In a spontaneous surge of joy, the three embraced, feeling an overwhelming sense of celestial love binding them together. As they stepped back, Johns, astonished by the warmth of the moment, remarked, "That was strange," marveling at how easily they had connected.

"I think it was perfect. But it's time we got out of here," Gunderson said.

Outside the cave, each took one of the pills using the water Beast had given them. After about five minutes, Johns' exhaustion evaporated. The way back to the Jeep no longer daunted him. He started toward the narrow passageway leading out of the box canyon.

Gunderson said, "There's another way out of here; it was how that hiker accidentally found the cave." He led them to a hedge of bearberry shrubs with thick, leathery, reddish leaves. He pushed through them and past several boulders. On the other side, a narrow trail wound upward through the boulder field to the top of the canyon. Heights normally bothered Johns, but with the pills and water he found himself moving with the grace of a mountain lion. Sarah moved equally well. From the canyon rim, Gunderson led them on a short hike across a rocky flatland to the other side. Johns and Sarah gasped in surprise. They were not far from the trailhead where the Jeep was parked.

"Christ, why didn't we come in this way?" Johns asked.

Gunderson smiled at him. "Your experience in the cave should be enough for you to know why."

Johns reddened. "Of course."

"Where's Beast?" Sarah asked.

"Taking care of our unwanted shadow," Gunderson said. The rumble of thunder cracked through the air. Clouds scudded eastward. Gunderson's face clouded with concern. "It's probably nothing, but I don't want to be caught out in a storm. Let's move."

36

BEAST

PINNACLES NATIONAL PARK

Francis Mellon settled on a rock forming a natural saddle by the entrance to the small crack through the talus boulders. He was by nature a patient man so did not panic when two hours passed and the trio hadn't shown up yet. The Dominican warned him a visit to the cave might take all day.

Mellon relaxed; waiting was the most perilous part of any mission. Waiting could make a man sloppy. He used the time to visualize how he would take out the three and gain the Eye. "Seeing clearly what you want to achieve is ninety percent of success," his Navy SEAL Commander advised.

His eyes were half slitted when he heard the scrape of a boot on rock. He came up on the balls of his feet, instantly on guard. Something about the sound was unsettling. It seemed forced, as if intended to get his attention. His hand reached inside his light coat for the Glock nine-millimeter he carried.

"Too late," a husky voice whispered behind him.

Mellon whirled, jerking the pistol from its side holster at the same time. A fist connected to his wrist, and the bones shattered. He screamed against the pain. Another fist slammed into the side of his head. He fell into blackness.

* * *

Mellon's eyes fluttered open. Pain lanced through his head. His wrist had been splinted and his arm put in a sling. He tried to move, but his stomach rebelled. He vomited onto his shoes. "Fuck," he muttered.

"Don't try to move. You have a concussion, and your wrist is badly hurt. You could lose the use of it if you fall."

Mellon looked up at the source of the voice. A bright nimbus of sun surrounded his tormentor's head. He winced against the brightness and turned away. The movement was too fast, and he vomited again.

The man *tsked.* "I said don't move." Mellon's assailant wiped the corners of his mouth with a paper towel then held a canteen to his lips. "Drink."

Mellon coughed; the rack in his lungs made his head spin. He fought down the nausea. "Thanks. What's your name?" he asked to give himself time to figure a way out of his predicament.

The man chuckled. "You can't escape, so don't waste your brain on trying to figure out how."

The pain in Mellon's head eased; perhaps something was in the water.

"You're right. I put a mild blood thinner in the canteen. It dilates the blood vessels in the head. There's also a mild stimulant— a little amphetamine. No worries."

"What do you want with me?"

"Answers."

Finally, Mellon could open his eyes without pain or nausea. The clearing was empty. His feet were bound and his good hand trussed behind his back. His shoes and socks had been removed. His attacker was a large man with a bald head and dark blue eyes. He radiated an intensity that went beyond anything Mellon had experienced training with the Navy SEALs. "You seem to know everything."

"My friends want to know what you know and why you're following them."

"I was out on a hike. You're facing a helluva lawsuit, friend," Mellon said, his voice steady. The drink had cleared his head, and he was thinking well. His bonds were too secure, so his only way of getting out of this situation alive was to bluff.

The man frowned and seemed disappointed. "I thought you were a professional and understood there's nothing you can do to stop me from getting the answers I seek. I guess we'll have to do this the old-fashioned way." He grinned. His teeth were white, the canines filed to sharp points.

Mellon flinched despite his training for situations like this. "So, what's next? It better be to call your lawyer and the Park Service ... in that order."

"My name's Beast, but don't let that fool you. I'm not a Russian goon or a Gestapo fanatic. I prefer interrogations that don't leave any easily identifiable marks." He reached into the pocket of his jeans and drew out a length of string. He tied it around the big toe and next toe of Mellon's right foot. He placed a sharp rock between the digits, looped a stick into the string, and twisted.

Mellon stifled a cry as the stone wedged tightly against his toes.

"I learned this trick reading *Flashman* by George MacDonald Fraser. Harry Flashman was the bully in *Tom Brown's School Days*, an English classic." Beast twisted the string a second time. The rock's sharp edges cut the soft skin, and Mellon bit his lip to keep from screaming.

"The tissue between the toes is incredibly tender, a lot of nerve endings, like there are on the fingers and hands. Did you know there are people who can play guitars with the toes? Now tell me, who are you working for?"

"You've got it all wrong, friend. I'm just a hiker."

Beast nodded. "Most people talk by the third twist. I'm pretty sure you're going to last to five. At six, you shit yourself. By seven, you'll beg me to kill you." He twisted the string two times quickly.

Mellon screamed, sure he would pass out from the pain.

Beast shook his head. "The stimulant in the drink is also meant to keep you from passing out. Now, tell me what I want to know." He turned the stick again, and Mellon shit himself.

37

———————

THE PROCEDURE

CHIMERA LAB

At 29 Palms Marine Base, Martin and his father returned to the Chimera Lab. Lance Corporal Henderson lay motionless on the hospital bed, monitors showing his vital signs steady.

"He's moderately sedated," a tall med tech said.

Martin inspected the PICC line, a long, thin peripherally inserted central catheter tube threaded through a vein in the arm and into the larger veins near the heart. He nodded approvingly. "Good. Get the other orderly and stand by."

The med tech saluted and left the lab.

Martin went over to a locked cabinet, punched in a code, and the door swung open. He pulled out a small medical device the size of an iPad. Martin motioned to his father to come over and look at it.

"This is my bioelectrical stimulator. It has a digital touchscreen interface I can use to program a pattern of signals to communicate with cell networks."

The general examined the multiple, disposable silver chloride deep cup electrodes extending from the control unit. "So, you put the pads on the skin, I presume?"

"We identified multiple nodes that are central points for control of many of the body's functions," Martin continued, "thereby influencing cell behavior and tissue development."

"Amazing." His father hefted the device. "Light and compact. I assume it's battery-powered?"

Martin nodded. "It runs on a fifth-generation lithium-ion battery. Portable solar panels enable it to be used in places where no power is available."

"Perfect for the final cave," the general said.

Peeling paper from the several self-adhesive leads, Martin attached one behind each of Henderson's ears, one on either arm, and the last one to the corporal's chest.

The general peered over his shoulder with keen interest. "What now?"

"Using the interface, I program a pattern of bioelectrical signals that tells the body's high-level control nodes to move into a deep state of dormancy, like a bear when it hibernates. In this case, what we've learned is that the body already knows how to do this; the beauty is we don't have to do anything or even know how it's done."

"How is that possible?"

"It's like the set point on your thermostat. The collective intelligence of cells does the rest. I'm activating the set point."

Martin pushed the send button.

The corporal's face remained placid while his breathing slowed. After three minutes, his breathing stopped completely. His heart rate plummeted to ten beats per minute, and then the EKG showed it stopped. The corporal's eyes fluttered as if in deep REM sleep, and the EEG measured normal brain electrical activity.

Martin checked the levels against the simulations. He gave his father a thumbs up. "So far, he's hitting all the points perfectly."

Five minutes passed. The EEG beeped. Martin stared at the readout, whose waveforms had become erratic. "That's odd," he said.

"What?" his father asked.

"The EEG is showing signs of an epileptic seizure." He waved at the med techs. "Get in here."

The corpsmen reached the bedside as the EEG's alarm went off.

Martin shouted, "Epinephrine and diazepam, stat!"

The tall med tech inserted a needle into the PICC line and administered the drugs. The other one attached a nasal cannula and turned on the respirator.

Shocked, the general asked, "What happened?"

"He had a seizure. I couldn't risk brain damage or damage to his heart." Martin pulled the stethoscope from around his neck and listened to Henderson's chest. "He's stable now." He turned to the med techs. "Stay with him." Hooking a finger at the general, Martin motioned his father to join him outside in the hallway.

The general wore a look of deep stress on his face. "This is not good; the whole project depends upon your procedure working."

"I know, I know," Martin answered calmly.

"What are you going to do?"

Martin threshed his sandy hair with both hands. "For starters, I'm getting away from here where I can quiet my mind. The solution will come to me."

The general jerked a thumb over his shoulder at the lab. "What about that young Marine?"

"He'll be fine. Those med techs have been part of my research team for a couple of years. They can handle it."

Martin walked out of the Chimera Lab. His father followed.

"Where are you going?"

"I think I know where the third cave is." Martin hopped into his Ford F-150 pickup, which was parked in a spot labeled 'Reserved for Dr. Davidson.' "You coming, Dad?"

38

LA COPINE

LANDERS, CALIFORNIA

The general sat at an outdoor table, watching his son in deep thought at the La Copine restaurant. The establishment was the only elevated, internationally recognized dining experience in this remote part of the Mohave Desert.

Gradually, a smile came over Martin's face. "I know what I did wrong, and it's an easy fix."

"You'll do another test?"

"I'll let you know when I wake up Corporal Henderson."

A strong gust of wind blew the menu off the table. With catlike reflexes, the general grabbed it.

Martin chuckled. "I saw Dr. Ravensbach do the same thing. You guys really are mutants."

"You were here with Simon? What did you talk about?"

"He was curious about my work and mentioned he had chosen a place near here where Prometheus is going to conduct the grand medical near-death experiment."

"Did he tell you where exactly?"

"No, he was going to, but then he was murdered."

"Simon picked the spot for the Sedona cave. He had a sixth sense about ley lines. He could physically feel the energy."

"You know, of course, there's no better place than right here with Giant Rock nearby and the mysteries surrounding George Van Tassel. The FBI even had files on him."

"I knew George." The general chuckled at the memory of meeting the ufologist who had lived beneath Giant Rock and later built a small community surrounding the landmark.

"What's so funny?"

"Tassel was a character. He'd start talking, and in the space of a couple of minutes he'd describe machines for which uses hadn't been invented yet. He was always ten steps ahead of everyone. Simon was the only one who could keep up with him, and even then, he was exhausted after a half hour." The general took a sip of coffee and set it down on the table with precise care as if marking the spot. "I think Tassel had a near-death experience but didn't know what to call it."

"Dr. Ravensbach told me the same thing. Said—" Martin stopped and looked away. "He'd had a number of conversations with George back in the day that pointed in that direction."

The general drummed his fingers on the table. The impacts made tremors in the coffee. The eddies settled quickly. "You were going to say something else."

"Dr. Ravensbach hinted to me he believed George's real purpose ultimately had something to do with Prometheus."

"There were claims George could see into the future."

"Anyhow, since Dr. Ravensbach was murdered, I've been poking around the area, and as I said earlier, I think I know where the third cave is. Can I show you?"

"Yes, but there's something I need to tell you. While I was driving here, I got a message from Gunderson that Dr. Johns was able to identify the chant."

Martin whistled. "That's huge."

His father nodded. "It confirms our decision that he be selected as the initiate."

"Excellent, but that isn't what you wanted to tell me ... is it?"

"You were always the intuitive one. There's a complication. After what happened at the Sedona cave, Johns became attached to Sarah Davenport."

"Dr. Ravensbach's daughter? Wow, that's more than a coincidence."

"For sure, although in retrospect, predictable."

"What do you mean?"

"You already know your mom was an initiate and died from cancer when you were four."

"Uh-huh. That's the main reason I went into regenerative medicine—so nobody like my mom would have to die like that again."

The general sucked air through his front teeth. "That's not the whole truth. Your mom was one of the designers of the Prometheus Project, and she chose to commit suicide."

"Christ!" Martin's fist slammed against the table, upsetting the coffee. He stood and walked away, staring into the desert filled with Joshua trees. Finally, he sat back down. "Why did you lie to me?" he asked, staring directly into his father's eyes.

"Betty was sure she could reincarnate. As you know, reincarnation is at the crux of the Prometheus Project achieving its goal."

"Fuck!"

"She reincarnated as Sarah Davenport. I feel Betty's presence every time I get together with Sarah."

"So that's why you always kept her from me."

39

GOAT MOUNTAIN

LANDERS, CALIFORNIA

The general and Martin drove north from the restaurant, entering an area in the Mojave Desert crisscrossed with tracks from many off-road vehicles that used this broad sweep of sand. Trail bikes and tricked-out vehicles looked askance at the Marine pickup. An all-terrain vehicle whizzed by, its occupants giving them the finger.

"Stop that man. I'll drive," the general said, pulling on Martin's shoulder.

The two men switched places, and the general chased after the ATV, driving the pickup like a stuntman, bouncing, flying, and spinning across the rugged sandy landscape. Eventually, they caught up to the ATV, which came to a stop. Embarrassed, Martin watched as his father approached the driver. But all the smiles and handshaking puzzled him.

Returning to the pickup, the general smiled. "Ex-combat veteran and his wife who did deployments in Iraq. All is good. They said the best trail to Giant Rock is over there." He climbed back into the driver's seat, and they took off.

"What's with the detour?"

"I want to show you something."

Off in the distance, they could see an immense landmark, the largest free-standing boulder in the world. As they closed on the rock, two things stood out immediately. Graffiti covered the lower reaches on all sides and fire scars told of giant bonfires that blackened the walls where they overhung the desert. Broken glass littered the ground.

The general pulled to a stop fifty yards away. He stared at the monument, grimacing at the graffiti marring the surface.

"What's wrong, Dad?" Martin asked.

"The history of this place has many chapters, beginning with the Native Americans who held it as sacred ground. To some, the magic in the rock represented the heart of Mother Earth. It is the perfect place to culminate the Prometheus Project."

"That's understandable. It sits right atop one of the strongest ley lines in California, right next to the San Andreas Fault."

The general put the truck in gear and circled the rock until he came to an area on the north side. He pointed at the ground, which had recently been filled in. "Beneath the rock were the living quarters of Frank Critzer, who excavated about 400 square feet of space under it and lived in the cool cavern year-round. He was a mentor of George Van Tassel, who lived here with his family for many years after Critzer."

Martin whistled. "Synchronicity abounds."

"That's not all. Both Critzer and Tassel died under mysterious circumstances. Critzer was killed in a dynamite explosion in his underground rooms on July 24th, 1942, when the local police raided his home."

"And Tassel died of a heart attack, even though he showed no signs of cardiac trouble."

The general nodded. "Like you said, synchronicity abounds."

"Indeed. Finding the trailhead to Goat Mountain is a little difficult. Let me drive."

Reluctantly, the general exited. They met behind the pickup. The general put his arm around his son. "Have you been able to process yet what I told you about your mother?"

Martin pulled a faded picture from his wallet, the edges worn from years of handling. In it, three-year-old Martin knelt beside his mother, her warm smile lighting up the moment as they breathed in the fragrance of vibrant irises. A flood of emotions surged through him, and he whispered, "My most vivid and enduring memory of Mom is an indescribable love. It envelops me again, so strong and ever-present, when I behold her image."

He glanced up at his father, and his heart ached at the tears streaming down his father's face, mirroring his own grief. Without a word, they embraced tightly, the weight of their shared loss binding them in a moment of silent understanding. When they finally stepped back, the air felt heavy with unspoken memories. They climbed into the pickup truck, the atmosphere still charged with emotion.

Finding the trailhead leading up Goat Mountain proved to be a challenge. There were no designated parking lots or side roads—just a stretch of hard-packed sand. After parking, Martin got out, the warm desert air washing over him, a stark contrast to the storm of feelings still swirling within. He grabbed two large Maglite LED flashlights and three twelve-ounce bottles of water, the weight of the backpack grounding him in the present.

He pointed to a large boulder ahead. "The trailhead is behind that rock. Interestingly, Goat Mountain is a lone protrusion rising out of the desert floor near Landers." As he spoke, his mind danced between the beauty of his childhood memories and the harsh reality of their current journey. The mountain loomed ahead, a reminder of challenges yet to come, and Martin felt the lingering presence of his mother's love, urging him onward through the bittersweet haze of remembrance.

They walked around the boulder and eyed the long climb to the top. The trail was little more than a goat path among the rocks and yuccas. A misstep and they would tumble down, a broken leg the least of their worries.

The general asked, "Is this necessary, son?"

Martin nodded. "I want to show you something and get your opinion before we look for the prospective cave."

He took off at a fast pace up the shoulder of the mountain. The general followed suit. The rocks and sparse vegetation pulled at them. Forty-five minutes later, they reached the top, chests heaving, legs aching from the rapid climb.

The top of Goat Mountain had been leveled and covered an area half the size of a football field. Laid out on the ground with the precision of a surveying team was a structure outlined by individual rocks with rock cairns at the cardinal points of the compass. Slowly, they circled the strange structure, stopping at each of the stone mounds and placing their hands on the rocks before moving on. When they returned to their starting point, Martin offered, "A creative sundial or medicine wheel, or perhaps a henge marking a portal for cosmic energy."

"We are on a ley line. I can feel the energy," the general said.

Pointing off in the distance, Martin said, "You can see Giant Rock and, farther south, Tassel's Integratron with its distinctive white dome."

"This is what you wanted to show me."

Martin said, "Yes. I thought you could answer a question for me."

The general straightened. "I think I know the answer without you asking the question. It's not random that Tassel and his Integratron lines up with Goat Mountain and Giant Rock."

"Right. These three points lie on the ley line that runs through California's Mojave Desert like an interstate highway."

"The third site Simon Ravensbach chose for the Prometheus Project has to be here." The general chuckled. "Let's look at that cave now."

The two men retraced their steps down the trail until they came across the remains of several old mine shafts surrounded by broken-down mining equipment.

"It is said," Martin began, "that in the '20s and '30s, brave souls prospected for gold here, and it's claimed that over 500 ounces of pure gold were taken back in the day."

"Hardly worth it."

"As you can see, most of the mines have been filled in over time, either for safety or because the shafts collapsed."

"So, you think what Simon found was an abandoned mine, not a cave?"

"I do. It's a possibility. Let me show you."

Martin led his dad to an area where medium-sized boulders appeared to be recently stacked. "Help me move these."

It didn't take long to reveal a mine shaft with cool air pouring out. Maglites in hand, they crawled through the shaft into a cavernous opening. Overhead, a single stream of light penetrated the dark. Using their lights, they examined the walls. To the untrained eye, the characters and figures looked like innocuous graffiti made of Greek symbols and numbers.

They high-fived each other.

40

THE FIX
CHIMERA LAB

General Davidson watched with intense interest as Martin attached leads to Adrian Henderson. The med techs assured the major the patient had suffered no damage from the first test and was stable. For his part, the lance corporal was eager to try again. They put him under with a light sedative.

Alone in the room with the patient and his father, the major began the procedure.

"What's different this time, son?" General Davidson asked.

"The first time the bioelectrical stimulator shut down too much of the corporal's brain's modeling system," Martin explained.

The general grunted. "What's the fix?"

"Instead of multiple electrodes, I'm using one electrode attached to the forehead and another electrode to connect to the third cellular command node in the heart region. Then a bit of reprogramming for the bioelectrical stimulator to not interfere with the body's nervous, respiratory and cardiovascular systems."

Martin pressed the send button.

As before, the corporal's face remained placid while his breathing slowed before it stopped completely. His heart rate slowed until the EKG showed it had stopped. Once again, the corporal's eyes fluttered as if in deep REM sleep, and the EEG measured normal brain electrical activity.

Seconds passed, and then minutes. Ten minutes went by. Martin checked the machine's readouts against the simulations. "We're five by five," he said. "I'm bringing the corporal's brain modeling systems back online now."

The EEG and EKG showed normal brain and heart activity. For five long minutes, nothing happened. Then the corporal stirred. After a few minutes more he sat up, groaning.

"How do you feel, Marine?" the general asked.

"Like I was run over by a Humvee. My fingers and toes are cold, and my skin is clammy."

Martin helped him sit up. "Here, drink this." He handed Henderson a glass of colorless liquid.

"What's in it?"

"A stimulant to warm up your body."

Henderson took a careful sip then drained the glass. He gasped, and his eyes widened.

Martin grinned. "I'm betting you're a little better than you were when we put you under."

"I feel great. What's in this stuff?"

"What do you remember?"

"Nothing at all. How long was I out?"

"About fifteen minutes total."

A tech, pushing a wheelchair, entered the room and approached the corporal.

"I feel fine. I can walk," Henderson insisted.

"Procedure," Martin said. He helped the corporal into the wheelchair. "He should take you to the debriefing room, but I want you to rest for at least two hours. Then we'll talk."

Once again, father and son were alone in the room. The general looked straight at his son. "We're right back where we started, aren't we? We don't know if it'll work or not."

"I could put him through this again, of course."

"This time, it'll be me. No argument from you, no sedative."

"I... I can't."

"We must know. No arguing." The general lay down on the medical bed. "Let's do it!"

Without a word, Martin attached one lead to his father's forehead and the other to his chest. He sat on the edge of the bed and began programming his device. A minute later, he pushed the go icon. Immediately, the general's face relaxed, and a slight smile crossed his lips.

"Will we be able to talk?" Martin asked, his voice trembling.

"We will see," the general replied as his eyes closed and his breathing became shallow.

Grabbing his stethoscope, Martin listened to his father's heart. Confident all was okay, he asked, "Can you hear me, Dad? Can you speak?"

No reply.

Martin waited fifteen agonizing minutes before bringing the brain modeling back online. Five minutes passed until his father's eyes popped open wide.

"Dad?" Martin asked breathlessly.

"That was incredible, son. I left my body. I saw you check my heart with your stethoscope. I saw the techs laughing with the corporal. Then I saw the base from the air, and then the whole planet, and the galaxy... Amazing. Just amazing!"

Martin deflated with a sigh of relief. "It worked. Your brain's modeling shut down longer than anybody else's in history."

"It was a wonderful out-of-body occurrence. After my near-death experience fifty years ago, I've wanted to return to that nonphysical realm one more time. Thank you, son."

"We're good to go?"

"Definitely." The general sat up and stretched. "I need to get to the base's airstrip. I'm on my way to Vandenberg for the rocket launch tomorrow evening."

41

THE SUPERINTENDENT

PINNACLES NATIONAL PARK

The drive back from the cave seemed much easier than the drive out. Johns still felt the effects of the amphetamines on his body and thinking. He couldn't stop visualizing the symbols on the cave walls and translating them. The words came effortlessly, and the chant, in ancient Greek, stuck in his mind like an earworm. As Gunderson drove, he encouraged Johns to repeat the letters.

Sarah stared out the window at the sere rocky landscape and late afternoon sun. Her thoughts disturbed her greatly. She could not let go of what happened in the cave. At the time, Gunderson and Johns were so engrossed by the symbols and their meaning they paid no attention to her. Gunderson had passed the Eye into her hands while he conferred with Johns, who repeated his understanding of the cave's symbols.

Holding the votive Eye in her hands and listening to Johns' chant sparked a retro precognition vision deep within her mindscape. She had, on multiple occasions, experienced retro cognition. However, this vision was unlike any she'd had before. She wasn't even sure it could have belonged to her. She had never been in the Pinnacles National Park cave before, yet the vision showed her in the cave on a gurney, holding the Eye, while a man standing beside her wearing an

Air Force lieutenant's uniform repeated the chant with her. In the middle of the chant, Sarah entered the woman's body and drifted off to sleep, though in her consciousness, the feeling was more as though she were dying.

What followed was as surreal as any dream but real in the sense that Sarah remembered doing everything that happened, not in a dreamscape, but in nonphysical realities. She stepped into a bright white light and emerged on the other side into a world of beings. One of the entities, without saying anything, reached out to her and welcomed her to the realm of the nonphysical.

She could have stayed there among the many beings watching time run on endlessly, but a different voice telepathically called to her. She stepped back through the white light and onto the gurney, where the man in the Air Force uniform kissed her forehead before taking the Eye from her. "Welcome, initiate," he said. The vision ended there.

Sarah replayed the vision in her mind as they completed the drive back to the park headquarters.

The parking lot was full when they drove in. Gunderson drove around the visitors center to the superintendent's office. In the back, they saw Beast talking with a young woman in her late twenties wearing a park service shirt tucked into dark green slacks. She had short auburn hair and a heart-shaped face with freckled skin.

Beast was talking animatedly. The woman pointed at a piece of paper he held and shook her head. They both looked up at the sound of the engine and stopped their conversation. Beast put a finger to his lips and walked away. He entered the building, leaving the woman alone to meet the others.

Gunderson hopped from the jeep and hugged her. "Good you could make it on your day off. Let me introduce you to Professor Isaac Johns and Sarah Davenport. Beth Kearny, Pinnacles' newest and youngest superintendent, and the person best qualified for maintaining the splendor of this beautiful piece of God's green earth."

They all shook hands.

Gunderson smiled. "Beth, could you show them where you live and some of the memorabilia? I'll be right over."

The superintendent shot him a quizzical look.

"Don't worry your brilliant mind any. Beast has something private for me." Slinging his backpack onto his shoulders, he trotted across the parking lot and disappeared into the office.

"What did Gunderson mean you're the best person for what I imagine is a thankless job?" Johns asked, hoisting his pack with the Eye onto his shoulder.

"He's being too kind. I wrote some papers on preserving the American condor. As a result, Pinnacles' designation was changed from monument to national park and set aside especially for breeding pairs. We've been successful in bringing the condor back from the edge of extinction. For that, they made me superintendent."

"Bravo."

"I knew your father," Beth said to Sarah as she drove to a large open field, well away from the visitor center. At the end of the blue stone walkway sat a small Craftsman built home. "One of the perks of being a superintendent," Beth remarked casually.

The tiny bungalow's cross-gabled roof with deep eaves provided shade in the hot climate of the Pinnacles. Beth told them the wood shake roof had been replaced with metal sheathing, as required after the disastrous 1991 Oakland firestorm, which destroyed more than 3400 homes and killed twenty-five people. Stained glass window panels adorned the top of the two front windows on either side of the entrance.

Inside, the building was as picturesque as a spread in *Better Homes and Gardens*. Oak floors glowed a soft yellow between built-in cherry bookcases and walls of maple wainscoting.

Sarah's eyes widened at the classic mission-style décor. "These are original Gustav Stickleys?" she asked, running her hand over an antique rocker with a cane seat.

Beth nodded. "You know your furniture."

"I worked summers at a high-end cabinet shop in Seattle. We

were often asked to make replicas of Stickley's signature chairs. Nothing like the originals, though."

"Another of the perks of being superintendent. Can I get you something to drink? It's a long ride back from the cave."

"You know about it?" Johns asked.

"I've been there several times. From the way Gunderson was smiling, I can only guess you helped him somehow."

Sarah said, "Isaac did. I only—" She was about to say, "came along for the ride" but that wasn't strictly true. From the moment of her father's death, she had been driven to uncover the secrets of his life and murder. The cave at Pinnacles and the one in Sedona held clues to what her father had been doing over the years—the long trips from home, clandestine meetings late at night in his study, and strange phone calls that took him away from the dinner table. And now her own vision after holding the Eye. "I only wish I knew more about this cave and people who started the Prometheus Project."

Beth's face brightened. "Of course, you both know about it. I'm a second-generation mutant like you, Sarah. I can tell when people are lying. That's my special skill," she admitted offhandedly with a laugh. "And you, Isaac, are special. I can tell ...." she laughed again. "I have pictures involving the cave and the early process going back several decades. Would you like to see them?"

"Would we!" Johns said.

"Yes, please," Sarah echoed.

Beth led them into a small room off the kitchen that served as a library. She pulled several picture albums from one of the bookshelves. "I have these scanned to my computer, but the originals show much more."

The superintendent opened the top album, titled *Pinnacles 1983*. The first picture was a group photo taken outside the cave entrance. Gunderson and Simon Ravensbach stood next to a young couple. Sarah recognized the man as the general in younger days.

She was momentarily taken aback by the youthful appearance of her father. His eyebrows were dark, bushy, and unkempt. His wavy hair didn't have any gray in it yet. His cheeks were clean shaven. She smiled.

The image of the young couple captured her attention. The general wore well-used outdoor clothing and was holding hands with a pretty, petite woman with dark hair drawn back in a bun. Her eyes were hazel, her nose turned up, and she had high cheekbones.

Sarah was acutely aware of her own hazel eyes and high cheekbones and how her nose turned up at the tip; she looked more like this woman than her own mother. "Who is that?" she asked, pointing at the woman.

"Betty Davidson," Beth answered. "This is her husband Deke, a captain in the Air Force at the time. She died about ten years after this picture was taken."

The vision from the cave returned to Sarah. The woman on the gurney and Sarah could have been sisters. *It was not a vision but a memory*, Sarah told herself. The revelation stunned her, and she stood staring at the late afternoon sun rays that broke into many colors through the home's stained-glass windows.

Her mind went blank for several minutes. When she came back, Johns was asking Beth about other pictures showing the cave's interior and the symbols on the wall. Someone had scribbled across the bottom of the album page תוספות. The script was indecipherable, yet it looked familiar. "What is that?" she asked, pointing at the script.

"Aramaic," Johns answered. "It translates as *Adonai*, the Hebrew word for God."

"Of course, but where's Gunderson?" she demanded of Beth.

"What?" the young woman said, taken aback by Sarah's vehemence.

"Where's the professor? He's supposed to meet us here."

"I'm not sure what you're getting at," the young woman said.

Sarah's change of tone caught Johns off guard. "What's going on?" he asked.

"Beth's distracting us." She turned on the superintendent. "Why?"

The superintendent settled back into her chair, a Mona Lisa smile playing across her lips. "Of course, as you know, two things can both be true; you needed to see those pictures."

42

THE PHONE CALL

PINNACLES NATIONAL PARK

Gunderson hesitated at the open door to the park superintendent's office. Curtains had been drawn across the open window, shutting out the late afternoon sun. Beast lurked in the shadows behind the desk.

"Close the door," he said.

Gunderson complied. He sensed Beast's unease but chalked it up to having killed the man tracking them to the cave. Beast might be an NSA Elite Team member, but taking the life of another human being still affected a person's psyche. *Be cautious,* he warned himself. He crossed the room but kept the desk between them. He wanted to turn on the lamp but thought better of it. Beast wanted the room to be dim.

"Did you find out who hired the man?"

Beast grunted. "I persuaded the operative to be... cooperative."

The dead flat tone in Beast's voice suggested he'd tortured the man. "Is he dead?"

"No. Francis Xavier Mellon is on his way to the Elite Team's headquarters. He could be useful to them with the right training." Beast slid a cell phone across the desk. "He had this on him. It's unlocked, and a number has been keyed in."

Gunderson picked up the phone. The alignment had changed in his partnership with Beast—he was no longer in control. *He's a younger initiate, and perhaps he seeks something different than we founders.* He pressed send. The phone on the other end rang.

* * *

The Dominican friar Augustus let the phone ring. He recognized the caller ID. *Mellon calling with good news,* he hoped, giving a prayer of thanks to Christ. On the fourth ring, he picked up.

"Yes, Francis," the Abbot said affably.

"Francis Xavier Mellon is no longer in your employ," the unfamiliar voice on the other end said.

Friar Augustus had received two great shocks in his life. The first when he nearly died at a young age. The second when he read Gunderson's paper on the Prometheus Project. The warmth drained from his face and his heart rate doubled. Mellon was an extremely capable man. He could only have been taken out by a Prometheus agent.

"You have me at a disadvantage, sir."

"Yes, I do. Mellon told us everything about your, and the Church's, interest in the Eleusinian school and the Prometheus Project."

The Abbot scrambled to give himself time to think, to figure out what to do. "I don't know what you're talking about—"

The man on the other end of the phone was relentless. "Don't bother denying what is common knowledge among initiates, Mr. Gallagher."

The Dominican stifled a gasp.

"Yes, I know who you are, Bill. So, let's cut the bull. If the truth got out about Jesus tripping out like some hippie pothead on shrooms—and that any person can have that same near-death experience—the backlash among Catholic followers would be devastating for the Church."

Friar Augustus grimaced. He tried to find advantages in the conversation. "Simon Ravensbach is dead."

"By your hand, no doubt," the man said.

"True. That leaves only three of the Prometheus Project founders alive. You're not Cynthia Apple or General Davidson. That means you must be Gerald Gunderson."

"Bravo. Your deductive reasoning skills are obvious for an initiate. However, you are in no position of power. Please give my regards to the Holy Father and tell His Eminence that the Eye is in good hands where it will not be used against the Church."

He's not a good liar. "I know what your plans are, but the Eye belongs to the Church. Turn it over to me, and you will be absolved of all your sins for creating this Prometheus Project abomination."

"Or, and this is my only offer, the Eye's existence will not be revealed as long as we're left alone."

The line went dead.

The Dominican stared speechless at the silent phone. The ultimatum was obvious. Gunderson had the resources to follow through on Prometheus.

"That did not go well," a gentle voice said from the other side of the office.

The Abbot bit back an angry reply. Gunderson had outplayed him, and he didn't need this whelp reminding him of it.

Janus Snyder stepped into a ring of light formed by an oval window looking out onto the garden. His manner was droll, but tension lines around his eyes showed his dismay at the Eye being so close at hand yet untouchable. "I can get it for you," he said.

Augustus sized up the young agent. The goal of the Roman Catholic Church had always been to acquire and destroy the critical artifacts of the project—the scroll containing the chant and the Eye. *This cocky young sod thinks he can do it.* "Mellon thought he could, too," he said, testing Snyder's resolve.

"Mellon didn't have my skills."

That's true, the Abbot thought. "I must contact the Holy See first. Meanwhile, stand down."

Snyder shook his head. "If the Pope decides to ignore Gunderson's threat, you're going to want me close to the action." He turned toward the door.

"Where are you going? I haven't dismissed you," the Abbot called out after him.

"To find Professor Isaac Johns and Sarah Davenport. They'll know where the Eye is."

Augustus watched Snyder leave. The plan to obtain the Eye was hanging by a thin thread. He needed guidance. He punched a button on the desk's intercom.

A nasal voice answered. "Yes, Abbot."

"The young priest bearing the message from the Pope, is he still here?"

"Yes. He returns to Rome tomorrow."

"He's returning to Rome tonight. I have a message to be delivered personally into the hands of Cardinal Sandrini of the Vatican Observatory. Bring him to me at once."

"Yes, sir."

Augustus cursed Janus Snyder and began composing the coded message.

43

THE ANODOS EXPLORER PROJECT

VANDENBERG SPACE FORCE BASE

General Davidson stood outside the squat, one-story control center for the SLC-4E launch complex at Vandenberg Space Force Base watching the preparation for the Falcon 9 rocket. This historic base had witnessed groundbreaking events since August 14, 1964, when the first Minuteman II intercontinental ballistic missile was successfully launched from the base. The location became particularly known for putting satellites into polar orbits. Later, SpaceX began launching rockets from Vandenberg in 2013.

Davidson drew a deep breath and sighed with satisfaction. After fifteen years of planning, the Anodos Explorer Project was finally coming to fruition.

"General?" A female reporter's voice interrupted his reverie. "Are you ready?"

He turned, noting the name on her visitor's tag, and gave his best smile. "Yes, Ms. Kelly."

Mary Ann Kelly was of medium height with bobbed red hair framing her elfin face. She looked outwardly frail, with pale skin and a petite frame. However, she had earned her position as CNN's chief NASA correspondent through merit, holding a PhD in astrophysics, and a reputation for asking hard-hitting questions. Her boss urged her to make the most of this rare opportunity. "You know something I don't?" she asked him before she boarded the chopper for Vandenburg.

"That's just it, Kelly," the balding producer said. "No one knows much about the Anodos Explorer Project. It's been highly classified. Find out whatever you can."

Kelly adjusted the green scarf around her neck, ensuring the light ocean breeze wouldn't whip the ends into her face. She turned to the cameraman. "Rolling," he said.

Settling herself, she decided to open with a comment to put the general at ease. "I'm here with General Deke Davidson, often referred to as the father of the Anodos Explorer Project. You must be excited, General."

"Excited and a little nervous," he replied. "However, the Anodos Explorer, derived from ancient Greek meaning 'ascent' or 'way up,' has been made possible by the hard work of many, many people working toward the common goal of putting the Von Neumann Universal Constructor into space, a self-repairing, self-replicating machine equipped with the most advanced argental artificial intelligence that will act like the brain of the Explorer.

"Kudos to you and your team, General." She paused, as if gathering her thoughts, though she already knew her next question. "General, 'anodos' can also mean 'pathless' or 'impassable.' So why are you spending all this taxpayer money on a secret project that was never officially approved by the U.S. government's space program?"

Davidson smiled expansively, prepared for this question. "The funding for the Anodos Explorer project is private. Plus, we are using SpaceX's rocket to deliver the payload into space."

"Are you aware that many religious leaders question the appropriateness of putting uncontrollable artificial intelligence into space?"

Davidson held back his amusement. He decided the best response was to inform her audience of Anodos Explorer's importance and the consequences for humanity if it weren't launched.

"Anodos employs sophisticated analog neural net technology, along with robust failsafe systems, to handle unforeseen situations without human intervention. That is the self-repairing, self-replicating aspect of the Von Neumann Universal Constructor."

Kelly faltered, caught off guard by his candor. "I ... I don't understand."

Davidson hid a smile at her discomfort and answered seriously. "There's no doubt about the serious crises facing humanity in the twenty-first century. In case one of the apocalyptic scenarios comes true, this is a way of preserving the essence of humans."

The general's statement mesmerized her. Kelly nodded and murmured, "Go on."

"The Anodos Explorer was engineered to reflect human capacities for imagination and creativity, a kind of ambassador for humanity, showcasing what we aspire to be at our very best—intelligent, ethical, and harmonious with the universe. Finding her voice again, Kelly replied, "That's interesting, but also alarming—like something out of a Terminator movie, wouldn't you agree?"

The general shook his head at the reporter's dramatic comparison. "There's no real danger here. As I said, the Explorer represents the best of humanity, not the worst. If there are other advanced civilizations out there, I'm confident they've made similar decisions."

Kelly nodded, caught up in the general's fervor. "Thank you." She turned toward the camera. "That was General Davidson at Vandenberg Space Force Base, preparing for an amazing space experiment that will soon begin right here. I am Mary Ann Kelly for CNN."

As the red light on the camera went out, Kelly removed her microphone and hurried after the general. With her background in astrophysics, she knew the implications of what the general had just discussed, echoing concerns that originated with the creation of nuclear weapons and President Reagan's Star Wars project. She caught up with him before he entered the launch complex's control center. "General, off the record. What you said back there. Is there a real chance for Anodos Explorer to survive in an apocalyptic event here on Earth?"

Davidson appreciated the genuine concern in her eyes. She was no dummy and no wide-eyed conspiracist. "It has to succeed, Ms. Kelly."

44

NEW MISSION

GRIFFITH OBSERVATORY, LOS ANGELES,
CALIFORNIA

Janus Snyder stood on the parapet surrounding the Griffith Observatory overlooking Los Angeles. As the sun set, the city came alive with lights, transforming the LA Basin into a glittering carnival. The observatory, with its iconic 1935 Art Deco architecture, was as recognizable as the Hollywood sign. For Snyder, this place represented both the future and the past; it was where he felt most at ease in L.A. However, tonight he was on edge, feeling out of place, much like Jim Stark in *Rebel Without a Cause*.

The confrontation with the Dominican left him feeling empty, as though all his choices led to a dead end. The Abbot's reluctance to seize control and pursue the Eye was a grave mistake. But without explicit orders to retrieve the stone votive tablet, Snyder felt adrift. Seeking divine guidance, he came to the observatory, hoping for a sign.

He waited for hours and was on the brink of losing hope when his cell phone buzzed. The caller ID was blocked. "Yes," he answered, his irritation evident.

"You're disappointed," came the dry voice of his handler.

"Angry," Snyder replied curtly.

"Indeed. Your mission failed. What did you expect?"

Snyder bit back an expletive. The shaman had interfered. Without the old Indian's meddling, he would have succeeded. "I can still get the Eye if I know where Isaac Johns and Sarah Davenport are headed."

"I believe you. However, the Eye is no longer the object of our search."

Snyder's heartbeat quickened. "I don't understand."

"I can give you another chance to do what your parents would have wanted—not Gallagher. I'll text you my address. Meet me here in an hour."

The line went dead.

Snyder stepped off the parapet and sat on the low wall, fuming. The mention of his parents irritated him deeply. He had spent years freeing himself from the grooming of their cult, and now his handler was trying to manipulate him by invoking their memory. Enraged by the blatant attempt, Snyder almost hurled his phone into the canyon below. He considered leaving the country, changing his name, and disappearing where no one from the Invisibles Academy could find him.

He let the impulse fade. He needed to find out what his handler wanted. His phone pinged, displaying the address. Google Maps estimated it would take fifty-five minutes to reach. He had time to research.

Using the white pages reverse lookup, he identified the resident of the address—Sam Hill. "Who are you?" Snyder muttered to himself. Employing all his skills, he delved deep, even into the dark web, to uncover everything he could about Sam Hill.

One thing was certain: Sam Hill, like his parents, was a member of the Invisibles Academy.

45

THE MISSION

PINNACLES NATIONAL PARK

Gunderson laid the phone on the park superintendent's desk. He didn't believe he'd put the problem with the Church and its obsession with the Eye to rest, but at least he gained them time. The Papacy would discuss his offer to Bill Gallagher for at least twenty-four hours before responding. By then, it would be too late.

He took several deep breaths and concentrated on the immediate threat. Beast had not moved from his spot in the shadows near the desk, hovering like a snake ready to strike, waiting for Gunderson's response. The gun Beth kept in the desk drawer wasn't an option. Beast would kill him before he could get to it. He had to find another way out of the predicament. *Toujours l'audace*, he thought. Always audacity.

"Beast, I need you to check our travel arrangements to 29 Palms Marine Base."

"Is there a problem?" the big man answered.

"The Church," Gunderson lied. "Gallagher will soon send his best man after the Eye."

Beast laughed. "Mellon was their best. I'm sure anyone else will be handled as easily."

"Which is why I need you to make sure our arrangements are

foolproof. I want a car to take us to San Francisco's airport. I've already booked tickets to LAX. Let yourself be seen, but don't be too obvious."

Beast raised an eyebrow. "You believe we're being watched."

"Of course. As you know, remote viewing is always the possibility. Los Angeles is a decoy. I'll drive to the base this evening after I've prepped Isaac and Sarah."

"Is it wise to drive if someone from the Academy is already onto you as you think they are?"

"Gallagher's assets will follow you." Gunderson checked his watch. "The four of us will meet at my home this evening just after dark. There, we'll make it look as if you're taking the three of us to SFO. Fifteen minutes later, I'll take our two young people south."

"Can you make it in time?"

"We need to be there no later than six tomorrow morning. We'll make it."

Beast pushed away from the wall. For a moment, Gunderson feared the big man had seen through the ruse, but he nodded and went to the door. "I'll see you tonight at your home." Beast waved mockingly as he shut the door.

Gunderson let out a breath of air. *Now for Isaac and Sarah.*

* * *

Gunderson waited until the superintendent left her home. The late afternoon sun streamed through the windows, but the AC hummed quietly, keeping everything cool. Noting Sarah's agitation and Johns' puzzlement, he smiled. "I suppose you're wondering what's next."

Sarah stood. She paced around the room once then turned by the stone fireplace and confronted Gunderson directly. "Just what the hell is really going on? This has been one big manipulation from the moment I agreed to go to Sedona."

"Indeed," Gunderson said. He sat down in a padded Shaker chair facing the two young people. "I need to tell you something. It's complex, so please sit and listen carefully."

He waited until Sarah took her seat by Johns. The two exchanged glances. Johns was filled with anticipation, but Sarah was not so impressed. Her gaze zeroed in on Gunderson, challenging him to provide a reason why she shouldn't walk out the door this instant.

Gunderson leaned forward, his fingers steepled, his voice calm but weighted with gravity. "Isaac," he began, "you have been chosen for a mission unlike any other. You are to be the first initiate at the new cave. But this is no ordinary rite. Tomorrow night, a rocket will launch carrying the Anodos Explorer, a Von Neumann Universal Constructor designed to replicate itself. If you accept, when the Explorer begins its journey into deep space, you will undergo a medically-induced near-death experience to allow your consciousness to transcend into the nonphysical realm."

The room tightened as his words sank in. Gunderson flicked his eyes to Johns, who was now holding his breath.

Gunderson continued. "You will be reborn into the Anodos Explorer, merging your pure human spirit with its technology. This will be the birth of a 'Technoeidolon,' a new form of humanity— where flesh gives way to machine but the soul remains."

Sarah's gasp broke the silence. She staggered back, as if the ground had tilted beneath her. The anger hardening her features for so long dissolved, leaving her face open and bewildered. "This... this is what my visions meant," she breathed. "I saw flashes of you, Isaac —flashes I could never explain... but they were always tied to something... otherworldly."

Gunderson's expression softened slightly, an acknowledgment of Sarah's understanding. "Your visions were a glimpse of what's to come," he said. "And they have guided you to this moment."

Johns, standing by the doorway, shook his head with a mix of disbelief and frustration. He had delved deep into the mysteries of the Eye, translated ancient chants that seemed to open portals to new dimensions, but this—this was beyond anything he had encountered. "Reincarnation into a machine?" he said, his voice tinged with incredulity.

"Not a machine ... the most highly advanced artificial intelligence matrix." Gunderson chuckled, a sound that carried more knowingness than humor. "Johns, you've already met your spirit guide," he replied, his gaze steady. "In the Sedona cave, when the veil between worlds thinned. He exists both here and in the nonphysical realm."

Johns recoiled as if struck, his mind racing back to the figure he encountered in the first cave. "That... shaman?" he stammered.

"Yes," Gunderson said, his voice echoing with finality. "And now, Isaac, you must decide. Will you be the soul of this new creation? The first Technoeidolon?"

Johns' heart pounded in his chest. The enormity of the choice before him was incomprehensible. He felt a pull toward the unknown, a magnetic force drawing him to the edge of something both terrifying and awe-inspiring. His voice, when he finally spoke, was barely a whisper. "What happens... if I say yes?"

Gunderson's eyes gleamed. "Then, Isaac, you will be reborn—not as a man, but as the first true fusion of human spirit and universal intelligence. A new kind of life that transcends flesh, time, and space."

The room fell into a heavy silence, as if it were holding its breath along with the souls within it. Each of them, in their own way, stood on the brink of something entirely new—each reaction deeply meaningful, marking the moment when reality itself shifted.

Johns' mind raced with Gunderson's revelation and the responsibility laid upon him. "I'll be dead?"

"Only your body."

"That's a big part of my identity."

Gunderson laughed again. "Only in the physical realm. Your true self is much bigger than your earthly mind can imagine."

"And if I agree?"

"A chartered plane will take us from Monterey to Palm Springs. A vehicle will be waiting to take us to the 29 Palms Marine base to stay overnight. We then prepare for the initiation."

Sarah asked, "What about me?"

"I believe Simon would want you to be there; the Prometheus Project was his idea from the beginning." Gunderson's gaze locked onto Johns. "If you agree, Isaac, we'll handle everything that comes with your death."

My death, Johns thought, the weight of the decision pressing down on him. A vivid image of Helene filled his mind—her dark hair framing a delicate face, a prominent nose above thin lips, and those striking amber eyes set against burnished copper skin. He recalled the date of that memory: October third, two weeks before she proposed to him. A smile tugged at his lips. "Will I see my wife?"

"Absolutely. She's part of our nonphysical clan. She'll be there to guide you."

Johns let the notion sink in. Gunderson hadn't specified what awaited him after merging with the Anodos Explorer, the groundbreaking Von Neumann Universal Constructor satellite. This was no ordinary task; it represented the pinnacle of human achievement—a chance to harness the essence of creation itself. He might never reconnect with those he loved, yet in that moment, a surprising clarity filled him. The opportunity to unite with the Explorer, to become part of something greater, tantalized him. The chance to see Helene again was everything he desired, a reward worth any sacrifice.

The answer surged forth, free of hesitation. "Let's do it."

He glanced at Sarah, who gave a reassuring nod.

"Good," Gunderson said, leaning forward and taking their hands in his. He turned serious. "There could be problems ahead... dangers from bad actors. But I can see both of you no longer have a fear of death. For me, when this is done, I will be able to return home, which has been calling me ever since I had my NDE."

"Home," Johns said, understanding "home" had never been Earth, nor a heaven populated by angelic beings, but a different place, perhaps another dimension, filled with all the illuminated souls. A Sufi prayer came to mind, and he repeated it silently. *Toward the one, the perfection of love, harmony, and beauty, the only being united with all the illuminated souls who form the embodiment of the master, the spirit of guidance.*

"Amen," he said softly.

46

———

WHEELS WITHIN WHEELS WITHIN WHEELS

MALIBU BEACH, CALIFORNIA

The two men stood on the ocean-side deck of Hill's Malibu home, listening to the soft rush of the surf against the beach.

Snyder turned to face the shorter man. His deep dive on Hill turned up surprisingly little. Sam Hill, a slight, man in his mid-sixties wearing light tan slacks, an open shirt, and black loafers, looked unassuming, ordinary. But Hill was a Hollywood legend, a showrunner with more hits to his credit than David E. Kelly. Rumor and conjecture surrounded the Hollywood mogul, but nothing concrete linked him to any covert or subversive agencies that could account for his early meteoric rise in Hollywood. Unless he'd contracted with demonic forces, his accomplishments came solely from raw talent.

Hill smiled, and Snyder detected nothing but genuine warmth emanating from the man. Perhaps his premonition of danger was just nerves.

Hill leaned casually against the wood post and steel wire railing that protected watchers from the twenty-foot drop to the rocky shoals beneath the deck. "I'm glad you decided to visit. There's a lot you don't know."

Snyder gathered himself together. Perhaps tonight was when rumor and supposition became hard facts. "Such as?"

"Ravensbach—the man you killed—Gallagher, and I go way back. Gallagher believed he could end the threat to the Roman Catholic Church after he got the scroll and went after the Eye."

Snyder frowned. "You aren't telling me anything I don't already know."

"True, but what you don't know is the truth behind the reason it was easy for him to manipulate you into using your special skills in his efforts."

An uneasy feeling crept up Snyder's spine that Hill was about to divulge something shattering to his sense of self. "Go on," he said, consciously bracing himself against the deck as if expecting a storm gale to swirl out of the Pacific and knock him over the railing.

"He played on your feelings about your parents, their beliefs, and their untimely deaths. Your parents did not die in an accident as was reported by the police." Hill let the sentence hang in the air like a slap in the face.

Snyder's brain reeled from the implication. "You mean they were killed… murdered?"

Hill nodded. "In a manner of speaking, but not by criminals. They allowed themselves to die so their spirit selves could reside in the nonphysical realm."

"You know this how?"

"I helped them leave their bodies."

Snyder's heart thumped. Without thought, his hand shot out, palm blade steel-hard, to crush the larynx of the man who killed his parents. Hill made a small circular motion with his left hand, like a priest making a benediction. The whip-like strike slowed and stopped inches from the mogul's throat. Snyder tried to flex his fingers, but they would not move. He tried to take a step forward, but his legs wouldn't respond. He stood helpless in front of the man who killed his parents. He had been right after all—danger lurked here. Little solace came from that fact if Sam Hill was going to kill him too.

The filmmaker shook his head. "I wouldn't waste your talents,

Janus, seeing as how you have used them to your advantage for many years, and I have use for them now." Hill took a step back. He flicked the fingers of his right hand as if brushing lint from a shirt sleeve.

The force pressing against Snyder vanished. He fell forward and would have gone over the cliff if he hadn't grabbed the deck's railing. The stainless-steel braided wire cut into the palm of his hand.

Hill handed him a white handkerchief. "Press this against the wound. It will stop the bleeding."

Snyder wrapped the cloth around his hand and clenched his fist. "What did you do to me?"

"Mutant capabilities aren't unique to the offspring of individuals who have gone through the ritual of an NDE. Those who have directly experienced the Eye and the chant possess abilities that are often much more remarkable. Mine is called effortless power. Over the years I have refined it until it merges with the flow of all things."

"Why tell me all this?" Snyder glared at him.

"Because for many years now you have harbored unnecessary anger toward your parents for the way they raised you. I believe you have referred to it as an 'oppressive Invisibles Academy upbringing.'"

Snyder clenched his teeth at the words coming out of Sam Hill's mouth.

"The children of initiates are mutants. We have learned that, like you, they never feel at home in the world. Without the experience of the world before initiation, they lack context. Your parents didn't know this when you were conceived, and it bothered them terribly."

Snyder's anger was crushing his heart. He had to let it go, or he would never understand what his parents had given up their lives for. He breathed in sharply several times, letting each inhalation and exhalation control his heartbeat until his rage dissipated and he was calm again. At the same time, the wound on his hand stopped throbbing, and when he removed the makeshift bandage, new skin covered the cut. "Go on," he said, not hiding his astonishment.

Sam Hill motioned to a pair of deck chairs on either side of a small brazier burning sandalwood. "Let me tell you, there's something bigger going on here. The real prize is a piece of technology invented by the son of General Deke Davidson that has the capability of transforming the world. A new kind of initiation will take place using this technology tomorrow night somewhere near the giant rock in Landers, California. The only person who knew the exact location was Simon. Gallagher thought he could put an end to the Prometheus Project and all future NDEs by eliminating Simon. He didn't understand the importance of the amazing possibilities of new technologies that will be available to us. We wanted the process to play out so we could grab the device they're going to use by tracking the chosen initiate, Isaac Johns."

Snyder arched his eyebrows. "We?"

"A consortium of highly-placed individuals in business and government who understand the new medically-induced NDEs can usher in a permanent golden age for the planet." His gaze raked Snyder up and down. "All along, I thought you would be the right person to handle this."

"Why would I do that?"

"If you succeed, we get the device, and you get the Eye for Gallagher."

"Why can't you get the device?"

Hill sighed. "Unfortunately, it is well protected in a secure facility at the 29 Palms Marine base. The only time it's going to be unprotected is when the general's son takes it to the initiation."

"I should talk to Gallagher about this."

"You should not."

Snyder heard the finality in Hill's words and didn't argue.

Hill got up and ushered Snyder into the house. He led Snyder through rooms that were decorated simply, showing nothing of the opulence the man could afford if he wanted. At the home's front door, Hill said, "We are connected now."

With a slight push on his back, Snyder stood outside. An ethereal voice in his mind said, *Let me know your decision by dawn.* What Hill said was true; his special role in this was something he had often felt from his parents.

47

REFLECTIONS

PALM SPRINGS AIRPORT

The Eclipse 550 microjet's top speed of 450 mph allowed the trio to reach Palm Springs International Airport in just under an hour after leaving Monterey Regional Airport. Although the cabin was small, John's six-foot frame did not feel cramped. He and Sarah even dozed for a few minutes as the flight paralleled the San Andreas Fault.

Originally a small regional airport, PSI had become an international destination in the early twenty-first century, attracting wealthy snowbirds wishing to escape the harshness of winter elsewhere.

Gunderson landed the plane expertly and taxied toward the Agua Caliente Concourse. He veered away from the main terminal into a private hangar. The doors closed behind them, and for a moment, the building was dark before the overhead lights came on. Johns expected Beast to meet them, but instead a slight Hispanic woman wheeled a small stair ramp to the plane. She disappeared as soon as the metal railings clicked against the plane's fuselage.

Gunderson checked his watch. They had twenty-four hours before the scheduled launch. "We're not in a hurry," Gunderson said, "but we don't want to dawdle either."

Each of them had packed a light, simple carry-on purchased in Monterey that stowed easily in small compartments above the seats; they retrieved these now. Gunderson led them out a side door to a private parking area. Using his cell phone, he remotely started a gray SUV in the corner near the gate.

He smiled and said with mock relief, "So far, the bad guys haven't caught up with us."

Realizing they were close to Zack's hideaway in the Mojave Desert, Johns pulled out the burner phone to call his old friend. Before he could punch in the number, Gunderson shook his head. "I don't want the bad guys tracking us," he explained. "That goes for you, too, Sarah."

Most of Johns' enthusiasm had dissipated during the long wait in the afternoon at Pinnacles before driving to Monterey. "Are there really people who want to prevent us from accomplishing what we're going to do?"

"Yes." Gunderson grew testy at Johns' whining. "That's why we must do the cloak-and-dagger shit." He pressed another button on his phone, and the SUV's rear door and passenger doors opened. "Stow your gear, and let's get moving."

Johns asked, "Where are we staying tonight?"

"It's been arranged for us to stay on the Marine base, which is near to where your initiation will take place."

Sarah shook her head. "No ... we shouldn't ... we can't."

Johns' eyes widened at the vehemence in her tone. "Why?"

Gunderson was more direct. "What did you see?"

Sarah hesitated.

He waved at her impatiently. "You fell asleep on the plane. What did you see?"

Sarah took a deep breath. "I had a precognition that something terrible will happen on the base if we're there."

"Then where do we go?" Johns asked.

Gunderson had not planned for this interruption. General Davidson had assured him the base would be the safest place to stay.

But he wasn't willing to dismiss Sarah's precog abilities. "I'm open to suggestions."

Sarah closed her eyes. She knew where they could go but wondered if it would be smart to stay there. After a moment's reflection, she decided it was the best alternative, though the impulse driving this decision was itself murky, like her precog dreams. There was a rightness to it, but she couldn't say exactly why. Opening her eyes, she said, "My father has a condo in Yucca Valley I still have access to. I propose we stay there. We'll pick up food and I'll cook a meal. There are two bedrooms and a pullout couch, which I'll be happy to sleep on."

Gunderson shook his head. "I'll take the couch. You two need a good night's sleep."

48

SIMON RAVENSBACH'S CONDO
YUCCA VALLEY, CALIFORNIA

In the early dawn, before the sun topped California's Little San Bernardino Mountains, Sarah woke from the recurring vision she'd experienced since childhood—a bright fire descending from the sky, burning everything on the planet to white ash.

The night had been unseasonably warm in the high desert of Yucca Valley, 3,300 feet above sea level. But in the minutes before sunrise, Simon Ravensbach's condo bore a slight chill. Sarah wrapped herself in the covers, trying to recall the fleeting images in the aftermath of the vision.

She first visited the condo with her father at age ten. He brought her here, to his secret hideaway, to celebrate his birthday. The weekend had been filled with excursions to local sites: Joshua Tree National Park, Giant Rock—once known as the UFO capital of the world—and the strange building known as the Integratron. Her father described the tall white cupola structure as a fusion of art, science, and magic. When Sarah questioned the fancifulness of his description, he invited her to sit with him inside the building for a "sound bath." During the experience, Sarah's nightmare vision of the earth blazed brighter than ever. The precognition event, as her father defined it, frightened her. He reassured her, "The human race will not perish," giving her the strength to live with the vision.

Sarah slowly unwrapped the covers and sat up. The most curious image to appear in the vision was General Davidson, whom they were going to meet this morning. She felt a profound love upon seeing him that extended beyond space and time. *That has never happened before.*

She sat at the edge of the bed. Sensing the excitement around what would be a momentous event for Johns, and humanity, she practiced a mind-clearing technique her gymnastics coach had taught her to reduce her fears and allow her to move with the flow of life. She breathed in deeply, pulling her belly against her spinal cord then released the air in a sudden rush. Repeating the practice three times, slowly, the ego-produced anxiety eased, leaving only openness in its wake. Her dystopian vision of the future no longer held her in its grip.

The first rays of sunlight filtered through the east windows of the condo. She relished the warmth against her closed eyelids and opened them. She had chosen this bedroom to rise with the dawn. She dressed quickly and went downstairs to the kitchen.

Gunderson sat on a stool beside the center island, eyes open. He did not see or hear her walk by, and if not for the slow rising and falling of his chest, she would have thought him dead. On the other hand, he wasn't sleeping either. From the strange straightness of his body, he must have been in a catatonic state.

She pulled a half gallon of grapefruit juice from the refrigerator and drank it directly from the carton. Swallowing the tart drink, she made up her mind to tell him, once he awakened from his meditation, about the coordinates her father had given her in his dying breath.

49

———

DISAGREEMENT

JOKHANG TEMPLE, LHASA, TIBET

The last rays of sunlight reflected boldly from the golden roof of the Jokhang Temple. In a final burst of brilliance, the sun vanished, taking the last vestiges of day with it. Darkness fell swiftly over the heart of Lhasa. Candles and oil lamps glowed through the windows of the monastery. Monks went about their timeless duties, preparing for evening prayers. Quiet possessed the vast complex.

In a small room deep within the temple, the Rinpoche prostrated himself before the bones of Siddhartha Gautama, gleaming under the oil lamps that burned continuously. He repeated the beneficent sutra then pushed himself to a kneeling position. The lama was eighty-seven years old. In his lifetime, he had watched the earth's descent into chaos. During the first quarter of the twenty-first century, that descent had quickened vastly until it seemed as if the nine billion names of Buddha had already been written down, ending the story of reincarnation on this planet.

He put those thoughts away. Gerald Gunderson asked that he prepare the inner sanctum for the arrival of the three masters of time slips. He agreed, of course, for he owed Gunderson for his help in the survival of the Tibetan people from the brutality of their Chinese overlords. But even without the favor he owed his old friend, he would have acceded to the request. He believed, as Gunderson explained, that the Prometheus Project and the Anodos Explorer project were humanity's best chance for the continued turning of the great wheel of life.

The air shimmered in front of the old lama. Gunderson appeared as a ghostly specter. The man's strong Nordic features gleamed blue. He grinned and said, "Thank you, old friend, for preparing the room for our meeting."

The Rinpoche bowed and stood in a flowing motion, belying his age. "I hope all is well. I will pray for today's launch to go perfectly."

"From your lips to God's ears."

The lama left, sliding the rice paper door closed behind him.

Two more silhouettes flickered, and the ethereal forms of General Davidson and Cynthia Apple appeared.

"I feel we must meet on this eve of the launch," Gunderson said. He told them what happened with Beast.

"Forewarned is forearmed," Davidson said. "Thank you." He turned to Cynthia, whose specter flickered as if agitated. "Did you see what happened?"

"Only pieces of what occurred at Pinnacles and your journey with your son Martin to the mine at the top of Goat Mountain. What have I missed?"

Without speaking, Davidson and Gunderson shared their thoughts with her. She nodded in understanding as the key points of the Anodos Explorer Project fell into place—Johns felt his soul's connection to the clan and the strong pull to join his wife and do what was necessary ... Martin's technology was more powerful than any hallucinogenic chemical had ever been ... Davidson's experience with the bioelectric stimulator demonstrated that... Simon's daughter agreed to help them.

Digesting all this information, Cynthia asked, "Does Sarah know Gallagher is responsible for her father's murder?"

Gunderson shook his head.

The blue glow of her astral being shook. "We can fail as a result of forces beyond our control."

"That has always been a possibility," Davidson admitted.

"Other circumstances could impede the success of the Anodos Explorer," Gunderson said.

Cynthia and the general were surprised to hear the worry coming from Gunderson. He had been the architect of the process; so far, his plans and contingencies had worked beautifully.

"What do you mean?" Cynthia asked.

Within the mutual trance, Gunderson directed a question to the general. "Regarding your out-of-body experience, you felt the joy of complete freedom, but you did not reach our clan in the nonphysical world. I believe it confirmed the necessity of the ritual's chant, the energy of the interconnected ley lines, and the Eye."

"Are they necessary?" Cynthia asked.

"Yes and no," the general replied.

Gunderson's skepticism came through the connection. "Something else happened, didn't it?"

"Yes. I got an insight, or a download, into the nature of anti-gravity that I could put to use in our space program."

"Just with the use of your son's device?" Gunderson asked, surprise rippling through his ethereal image.

Davidson nodded. The spectral light made his wild mane of hair float about his head like a halo.

"Something else could interfere," Cynthia said. "Why is Sarah still in the mix?"

"It has to do with Simon," Gunderson answered. "Do you not feel his presence now?"

"Of course I do," she said sharply. "It was like he was saying she holds the key to success."

"There is more to her apocalyptic vision," Gunderson said.

"Speaking of success," Cynthia continued, "what do we do if everything goes perfectly?"

"Are we not agreed this is the end of Prometheus?" Gunderson asked.

"Does it have to be?"

"It is for me. I'm returning home to the nonphysical world once this is over."

The other two could feel his weariness at being trapped in the physical realm.

Cynthia felt her own weariness at the conversation. "Hasn't the Prometheus Project also accelerated the merging of human experience and technology into a new form of life? Doesn't your experience, General, indicate the downloads should continue at an ever more rapid pace?"

The time slip broke abruptly, and the room emptied as back in Santa Barbara, the general received an urgent message.

50

NEW GO TIME

VANDENBERG SPACE FORCE BASE

At 0700, the squat, one-story flight center for the SLC-4E launch complex at Vandenberg Space Force Base was a hub of frenzied activity. Banks of large LED screens manned by twenty individuals monitored the prelaunch vitals of the Von Neumann Universal Constructor Explorer. A screen larger than the rest dominated the center of the far wall and provided a panoramic view of the SLC-4E launch pad. A light gray fog of subcooled liquid methane and subcooled liquid oxygen hid the base of the Falcon 9's Raptor engine, a technology that enabled recovery and reuse of the rocket components. The Explorer was programmed to investigate new regions of space and possibly even different celestial bodies, replicating itself to continue the exploration on a larger scale.

Leaning against the yellow-striped railing separating the viewing and command areas, General Deke Davidson watched the two flight controllers who would communicate and command the Exploder's launch and activation. The younger of the two independent contractors leaned back in her chair. She had a dark, handsome oval face, cropped black hair, and piercing brown eyes. Multiple studs in each ear gleamed in the blue light from the monitor in front of her. Her nametag read *Proxmire*. She pursed her lips. "General, are you sure this is what you wish to do?"

"Yes," he answered, his face lined with weariness. He had gotten off the phone with the launch director and military supervisor, Harry Litmus, ten minutes ago.

"There's a new atmosphere of distrust between the Russians, the Chinese, and the US," Litmus explained. "Intel says the Chinese are planning something this evening. So, we should not be launching anything at the same time. What's so goddamned important about the Explorer anyway?"

Davidson squared his jaw. "Harry, I can't tell you. Not because it's above your pay grade but because that payload out there is the answer to Armageddon. And it's gotta get off the ground."

Harry grimaced and threshed his graying hair with a large, knuckled hand. "Copy that. This afternoon, thirteen hundred, is the best I can do, Deke."

The general studied the two women. According to Litmus, they were the best private flight controllers in the business. Both had flown fighter drones for the USAF before retiring and going commercial. "The more important question is can you do it?" Davidson asked.

The women looked at each other then nodded. Proxmire said, "We can do it, sir."

Davidson smiled. "Get it done!" He followed the ramp to the gallery overlooking launch control and headed for the double doors leading outside. Pulling out his phone he punched in the number for a burner phone.

The call answered before the first ring ended and a cautious voice said, "Good news?"

The general smiled at his son's temerity. "It's a go, Martin, but the time has been moved up."

All caution flew out of Major Davidson's voice, replaced by anger. "Shit. When?"

"Thirteen hundred. Can you do it?"

"We don't have a choice. Do Gunderson and the others know?"

"Gunderson is my next call."

"It'll take forty minutes to climb to the mine," Martin grumbled. "Tell them to meet me there at 11:20."

"Good luck, son."

"Good luck on the launch, Dad."

The call ended. The cool ocean breeze blew steadily across the base. The clear sky boded well. He thought about his idea for the antigravity device. So much could be done with it to help the world. *If only we get the chance.*

51

CHANGE OF PLANS
SIMON'S CONDO

The time slip ended abruptly, yanking Gunderson back to the present with a force that sent him crashing from the kitchen stool to the cold tile floor. He barely managed to brace his fall, his wrists aching as he pushed himself to his knees. For a moment, the room spun, and he gripped the edge of the kitchen island to steady himself. A sharp pain sliced through his temples, remnants of the mental strain from the abrupt termination of the meeting. Davidson's last thought still echoed in his mind, hurled at him with desperate force, to conceal the truth from Cynthia. Whether it worked, he couldn't be sure—Cynthia had been connected to both of them throughout.

His cell phone rang at 7:13 a.m. Caller I.D. said General Davidson.

"Gundy, is everyone okay?" Davidson asked.

"We're all set."

"There's a change in plans. The launch has been moved up to 1:00 p.m."

"Damn."

"Martin needs you all out at the site by 11:20. Can you make it?"

"We'll have to." The line went dead.

If Cynthia had betrayed them, and if she was remotely-viewing

Davidson, she might already be planning to send the Beast to intercept the bioelectric stimulator. He had to act now.

He strode to the stairwell and bellowed, "Wake up! Plans have changed. We're leaving!"

Within fifteen minutes, Sarah and Johns sat on the couch in the living room, their eyes tracking Gunderson's frantic pacing. The room, warm with morning sunlight streaming in through the windows, was a stark contrast to the tension thickening the air. Family photos adorned the walls, capturing Sarah and her father during their past visits to the desert. A large stone fireplace loomed over the room, an enlarged photograph of Sarah and her father in front of the Integratron hanging above the mantle.

Gunderson stopped suddenly, his fierce gaze locking onto them. "No time for breakfast," he said, voice tight. "We're heading to Goat Mountain. Now."

Johns frowned. "Why the rush?"

Gunderson's face betrayed a flicker of surprise before he quickly masked it. "The launch has been moved up to 1 p.m. The reincarnation needs to occur exactly when the Von Neumann Universal Constructor activates. It's like a birth—timing is everything."

"Hold on," Johns said, his voice hardening as he leaned back, crossing his arms. "You're not telling us something, Gerald. What's really going on?"

Gunderson exhaled sharply and sat down on the stone lip of the fireplace. "Those forces I warned you about... they may have figured out where the initiation will take place. We don't have the luxury of time anymore. We need to move."

Sarah's brow furrowed. "But we don't even know where the initiation is supposed to happen."

"On Goat Mountain," Gunderson replied, already rising. "An hour from here plus a hike. The earlier we get going, the better."

Johns got to his feet, but as he did, Sarah's eyes fluttered shut. "Sarah?" Johns called, reaching out to touch her arm.

Her eyes snapped open, and she drew a sharp breath. "I'm fine," she said, though her voice was distant. She turned to Gunderson, a sudden clarity in her gaze. "The numbers... the numbers my father made me memorize before he died—they're coordinates. I didn't know what they meant then, but I checked last night. There are three sites near the longitude 116°24′13″W that could be significant: Giant Rock, Goat Mountain, and the Integratron."

Gunderson's expression tightened as he processed the information. "It could be any of those places," he said. "But Davidson and his son are certain it's Goat Mountain. That's where we'll go. But stay alert. We can't afford any mistakes."

Sarah's eyes narrowed. "Something feels wrong," she whispered, a tremor in her voice.

Gunderson's gaze sharpened. "Do you have anything more concrete than a feeling?"

She looked past him, as if searching the air for answers. "I don't know... it could be the place, the timing, or..." her voice dropped to a whisper. "The people involved."

Gunderson glanced at his watch and scowled. The time was slipping away, and they still had a narrow window to reach Goat Mountain before the launch. There was no more room for hesitation. "We don't have time to figure it out. Get your things. We're leaving now."

Sarah hesitated only a moment longer, her gaze sweeping the room. Her eyes fell on the photograph above the fireplace—she and her father waving at the camera outside the Integratron. She couldn't recall who had taken it. Her mother had died the year before, and she'd never met any of her father's colleagues. Perhaps it was one of the Integratron's owners—they had always been more than welcoming, as though they were somehow in on the secret.

On a whim, she took a picture of the photograph with her phone before heading upstairs to grab her travel pack.

As she approached the front door, a shiver coursed through her, and a heavy sense of finality settled over her like a veil. She realized, with startling clarity, that she would never be coming back here.

52

ANOTHER MAN'S DREAM
MALIBU, CALIFORNIA

From the wide deck at the back of his Malibu home, Sam Hill watched the Pacific Ocean swells roll lazily onto the beach. Froth splashed against the rocks. A fine spray coated the railing and the first few inches of the Ipe planking. Early morning sun cast jewels across the water. He took a sip from the mug of fresh coffee and sighed, savoring the subtle earth tones in the arabica beans roasted especially for him. He took little pleasure in accumulating material things, such as cars and homes. Personal tastes in food, wine, and coffee brought him a deep pleasure, though the real reason for joy and purpose in his life was producing movies and series with his new style of science fiction that triggered the imagination of the masses as well as the scientific community. He wondered wistfully how much longer this could continue.

"You're sure?" he asked, directing his gaze to the visitor who had shown up on his doorstep a hair before sunrise.

"As I told you on the phone, I saw enough to know the launch is scheduled for 1 p.m., and the initiation will take place on Goat Mountain. Not to worry, my old friend. I was able to see him call Gunderson."

Hill sighed. "I never did master nonphysical communication."

"You have other abilities ... like effortless power."

Hill turned toward the speaker.

Cynthia Apple leaned against the deck chair's cushion. Her eyes never left his. "Will the young mutant help us?"

Hill nodded. "I turned Snyder around. He was genuinely surprised to learn about his parents."

"Did you tell him the entire story?"

"I did. He would have seen through a lie."

"Good." She smiled slyly. "Did he attack you?"

"He tried." Hill laughed. "It was perplexing for him."

Cynthia sipped orange juice, appreciating the fresh taste. "You have always set a good table, Sam. It's why I agreed to help you."

"You're not talking about the orange juice."

She laughed. "What now?"

"I let Beast and Snyder know where the rendezvous is to take place. They'll take the device from Martin Davidson and bring it here."

"And the Anodos Explorer Project?"

"There's no reason to stop it from going forward. The Von Neumann Universal Constructor doesn't interfere with our goal of using Martin's invention to accelerate the download of new knowledge. Besides, what if the general is correct and the world is moments from being destroyed because we're too late to find a solution to the technological bottleneck that has destroyed many galactic civilizations?"

Hill set his coffee down on the glass-topped table between the deck chairs. He pulled his phone from the pocket of the robe he wore against the morning chill drifting off the ocean. He punched in two numbers and spoke rapidly. "Goat Mountain at one this afternoon. Wait until after the launch. Secure the device. Harm no one unless necessary." He glanced at Cynthia for approval. She nodded. He pushed send, and the text disappeared with a whooshing sound. He waited, holding the phone with an air of excited expectancy. Two pings followed close together. He smiled. "It's a go."

He sat on the chair and picked up his coffee. Leaning across the low table, he clinked glasses with Cynthia. "To success for everyone."

The end of Cynthia's lips twisted downward into a sad frown. "I wonder how many more sunrises will be observed by humans?"

Hill nodded thoughtfully. "That is what we're trying to save." He gazed out at the horizon, melancholy seeping into his musings. *Ever since the ancient Greeks, humanity's pursuit of truth, goodness, and beauty has driven us forward. But what if that pursuit leads to our downfall?*

He took another sip of his coffee, the rich flavor doing little to soothe the weight of his thoughts.

53

———

EPIPHANY

JOSHUA TREE NATIONAL PARK

Janus Snyder came alert immediately at the text notification. He read Hill's message and sent back the expected response—a thumbs up emoji. He rolled out of the sleeping bag and stood. He'd slept outside without a tent, preferring to watch the night sky wheel above him with its thousands of stars and constellations easily seen in the clear desert air of Joshua Tree National Park.

The dry, cool, early morning refreshed him. He rolled the text through his mind, paying attention to the last sentence, especially. "Goat Mountain at one this afternoon. Wait until after the launch. Secure the device. Harm no one unless necessary."

"Unless necessary," he muttered. In the beginning of his quest to find the Eye, "Harm no one" had not been a part of the Church's orders. The Dominican Abbot impressed upon him the votive stone must be obtained at all costs. For him personally, evening the score with the Invisibles Academy had been enough to spur him to succeed.

Interestingly, he had failed—and not from his own deficiencies but from outside sources. The shaman thwarted him at the cave outside of Sedona. He suspected he was being herded toward an outcome. *But what outcome?*

No answer presented itself, so he proceeded with the morning ritual that had sustained him during the Iraq War. For ten years, the Gnostic Warrior ritual had awakened his body every morning for the rigors of combat. His fight was no longer in the Middle East, but the current battle was even more honorable.

Pulling a leather-bound bundle from his backpack, Snyder laid the package reverently upon an improvised altar of stones gathered from the desert. Methodically, he unwrapped the contents, laying each fold precisely to the side until fully revealing the sacred object. He gazed fondly upon a *xiphos*; the one-handed short sword used by the ancient Greeks. The Iron Age blade was thirty-six centimeters long and double-edged, with a long narrow point. The twelve-centimeter oak handle fitted his palm perfectly. The weapon had been found at an Eleusinian site remarkably preserved.

He bowed to the blade.

As he recited the ancient Gnostic prayer for going into battle, he envisioned what the incantation evoked. "I am encased in the armor of divine light. No harm can penetrate; no fear can break me." He picked up the *xiphos* and held the ancient weapon to the sky. "By the power of the divine and the wisdom of Athena, I bless this weapon. May it serve as an instrument of justice and protection." Setting the short sword once more upon the altar, he gathered all his breath, and in a final cleansing *kiai*, shouted, "I am a warrior of light and truth. I carry the wisdom of the ages within me."

Swirling energy of the divine spun through him, and he felt his body floating as in a flying dream. Snyder gloried in the boundless depth of pure light. He opened his eyes and looked upon the vast space of spiraling energy. He had entered the nonphysical realm, where his parents' souls resided. Two bright specks moved toward him. For the first time since his parents died, he felt their presence as they embraced him with love. Without words, they said, "Come home."

At the height of the rapture, a gust of wind blew past. Not from the desert but from an unseen source. Snyder reentered his physical body and fell onto his side. He knew a great truth beyond all words. Tears filled his eyes, and he wept for joy at finally identifying his true home.

54

SARAH'S TRUE IDENTITY

YUCCA VALLEY

Gerald Gunderson drove a few blocks from Simon's condo with Sarah in the passenger seat and Johns in the back. He pulled into a convenience store parking lot and followed a narrow alley around back until they were out of sight from the main road. Pulling out his phone, he punched in Davidson's number. The general's craggy face appeared on the screen.

Gunderson said, "We have a problem. I've been trying to reach Cynthia, but she's not responding."

The general replied, "Me too. This doesn't feel right."

"What can we do?"

"For now, we continue with the plan. Martin's device is safe on base."

Gunderson turned toward Johns and Sarah. "And the three of us?"

"They won't come after you. It's Martin's invention they want."

Gunderson nodded. "There's one more thing."

"Sarah needs to know the truth before she meets Martin," Davidson interjected.

"Does Martin know?"

"I've already told him."

Gunderson handed the phone to Sarah.

She looked at the familiar visage on the tiny screen, relieved and strangely comforted to see him. "General, I—"

He cut her off with a laugh. "Call me Deke, luv."

Sarah jerked in surprise. An odd sensation washed over her. It started as the slight dizziness familiar from her prior altered states, but this time the sensation ran deeper, shook her more profoundly. She tried to steady herself by placing a hand against the door of the SUV, but the world around her blurred. A rush of memories that weren't her own—images, emotions, and thoughts—cascaded through her mind, overwhelming her senses. She struggled to hold onto her own identity, but the force was too powerful. The onslaught of feelings ran like a torrent that would go on forever. When she expected to pass out, everything went still.

Sarah opened her eyes, and though they were hers, they were now shared with another presence. The other person's awareness guided her movements, influenced her thoughts. Though she was no longer alone in her body, she retained enough of her own consciousness to realize with whom she shared her body and mind—the general's dead wife.

She stared into the phone with a loving appreciation for the man staring back at her. "Deke—" The name rolled off her tongue with a wonderful intense love that coursed through Sarah's body.

"Sarah?" Johns' distant voice echoed through the fog of her mind.

She turned to him. "I am here," she said, her voice a blend of her own and Betty Davidson's—familiar yet foreign.

Johns' eyes widened. "Sarah, what's happening?"

The presence within her grew stronger. Memories from another life flooded her consciousness: a life lived long ago, with different experiences, different people, and different knowledge. She was seeing the world through the eyes of someone else, someone who had once lived and breathed, someone whose essence now intertwined with hers.

"I... I remember," she said, her voice trembling. "I remember everything."

Johns reached out to steady her, his touch grounding her in the present moment. "What do you remember?"

"I am... I was..." she struggled to find the words. The other person's identity was merging with hers, making it hard to distinguish between the two. "I was Betty ... I am Betty."

Johns' face paled. "Betty who?"

"She is here, within me."

55

MAJOR DAVIDSON ACTS
29 PALMS MARINE BASE

ajor Martin Davidson punched "end call" and took a deep breath. He grabbed the backpack sitting on his desk holding the bio-electric stimulator and two mini solar panels to charge the lithium-ion battery if necessary. "It's go time," he said aloud. He checked his watch; 0900, four hours until launch. Plenty of time to get to Goat Mountain. He surveyed the Regenerative Bio-Electrical Lab. Everything was normal. Technicians went about their daily routines in the cell research lab. Anyone inquiring about him would be told he was somewhere on base.

Martin exited the building and walked toward the mess hall. Inside, he detoured from the line of officers queuing for coffee and headed toward the bathrooms. He passed them by and exited the rear of the hall. In less than a minute, he covered half the distance to his real destination and hopefully made it difficult, if not impossible, for anyone to follow him. He didn't like the cloak and dagger steps, but ever since Gunderson called with the revelation that Beast could no longer be trusted, he took every precaution possible so the Anodos Explorer Project would succeed. He looked behind him to be sure no one followed then jogged toward his real destination.

The Marine Corps Air Ground Combat Center at 29 Palms had

three gates for access. The main gate was located through Adobe Road 1. Additionally, a visitor center near the main gate was open Monday to Friday from 0500 to 2030, except on holidays. The third gate, located at the rear of a rusted Quonset hut, was a clandestine egress known only to a few Marines.

Martin felt as if he were using a secret underground passage in an ancient castle as he threaded through the haphazard collection of crates and machinery stored in the hut. Swiftly and efficiently, he disconnected the alarm system. He felt guilty at leaving the exit unguarded, but the Anodos Explorer Project was humanity's best hope for escaping the Great Filter Theory that civilizations had a bottleneck once they achieved a certain technologically advanced state.

The Bell 206 MedVac-Helicopter was waiting for him as his father promised. The two-seater craft was another misdirection. It would appear as though the pilot and a doctor were on their way to rescue someone hurt in the desert.

The flight was quick, and the pilot didn't make any small talk, which Martin appreciated. He was keyed up with the importance of the project and his part in it. Twenty minutes after leaving the base, the pilot pointed to the immense landmark in the Mojave Desert, and in two more minutes they landed. Martin nodded at the man, jumped out, and waited until the pilot took off and was no more than a speck on the horizon. He jogged the hundred yards to the secluded campsite he had set up the night before near Giant Rock.

Accessed through the mine at the top of Goat Mountain was the starting point for incarnating a human consciousness into the Von Neumann Universal Constructor. The whole area had a long spiritual history, as it was sacred ground for Native Americans. Like many before him, Martin found himself slipping into an altered state of consciousness as he thought about meeting Sarah. Within seconds, the unconditional love of his mother embraced him. The sensation had showed up for him periodically his entire life. His father told him it was because he was a second-generation mutant. He was relieved to feel it now.

After pulling the camo tarp from the dirt bike, he checked to make certain everything was in working order. The tires were inflated and the gas tank full. At forty miles an hour, it would take him five minutes to reach the Goat Mountain trailhead. Checking his watch, he saw he had plenty of time and could cross the sandy wasteland leisurely. He stashed the backpack containing the bioelectric stimulator into one of the dirt bike's panniers. The other one held a gallon of water. No one went into the Mojave Desert without plenty of water.

The motorcycle started easily. Martin smiled. *Almost there.*

56

———

UNLIKELY COMRADES

GIANT ROCK

Janus Snyder adjusted the binoculars and watched the dirt bike recede into the distance, headed on a straight line to Goat Mountain, the single prominence in this part of the Mojave Desert. "Just as Sam Hill said," he remarked to the man beside him. "He's going to Goat Mountain."

The man snorted. "We're wasting time here."

"I like to be thorough. It's how I stayed alive in Iraq."

"We should have taken the stimulator from him now."

Snyder glanced at his companion. Beast, an original Prometheus Project initiate, was six inches taller than him and broader in the shoulders and chest. His dark face was unmarred by any scars, unusual for a man who had been in as many fights as Beast's legend told. *Formidable ... and dangerous*, Snyder thought, though he sensed no direct danger aimed at himself. Still, something in Beast's demeanor suggested the man was not entirely on board with Sam Hill's mission to acquire the device.

He told Beast, "Hill was clear. Let the Anodos Explorer Project succeed then take the device."

Pocketing the binoculars, Snyder climbed into the jeep where Beast waited behind the wheel. Beast gunned the engine.

"Slow your roll," Snyder cautioned. "We have plenty of time to set up the ambush when they come down the mountain."

Beast grimaced.

Snyder smiled.

They pulled out. Snyder kept his thoughts to himself, but more than ever, he wondered if Beast had made other plans. He felt the *xiphos* nestled beneath his left armpit suspended by a leather thong.

57

—————

FINAL PILGRIMAGE

CALIFORNIA HIGHWAY 247

Johns sat quietly in the back seat of the vehicle as the trio began the drive along Highway 247 to Goat Mountain. He had not eaten or drunk anything since midnight. Reflecting on his recent journey to the caves at Sedona and Pinnacles, he quietly joked, "It seems I've done this before."

Gunderson nodded. "It's part of the protocol that originated twenty-three hundred years ago in ancient Greece when initiates made their way to Eleusis."

"As you reminded me at Pinnacles, exhaustion has always been a part of the journey to the nonphysical."

When they reached the halfway point, steadily climbing toward Landers, Sarah looked back at Johns. "You're going to be okay. Create an intention for success."

"I'm a little worried about you," he said, his concern evident.

"I'm anxious about meeting Martin," Sarah admitted, "but I feel fully myself again. I needed to merge with Betty's memories to understand our goal—yours in particular, Isaac."

"I like what I'm hearing," Gunderson said, nodding encouragingly to Sarah.

She continued, her voice steady and filled with conviction. "Isaac, your purpose is to embody your higher, nonphysical self in a new form—a non-biological medium, liberated from the limitations of sexual reproduction and the instinct to define others as enemies for survival. These patterns lie at the root of all human conflict."

Gunderson interjected, his tone carrying a sense of reverence, "The Von Neumann Universal Constructor is exactly that kind of medium. The technology being launched today is not the work of any single mind. It's a collective creation, shaped by countless downloads from the nonphysical realm. We've all played a part in its development, though no one fully grasps its totality. Yet from my near-death experience, I know this much—this is a step in fulfilling the grand purpose of the One of infinite potential."

A profound realization spread through Johns, as if he had glimpsed a hidden truth. This was more than just a technological leap; it was a new phase in the evolution of consciousness itself—a journey that began the moment life emerged on Earth. He was about to become part of a new paradigm, one that transcended the old divisions.

As Gunderson turned off Highway 247 onto a gravel path, the vastness of the Mojave Desert opened before them. The vehicle glided across sandy stretches of BLM land, the surface marked by the crisscrossing trails of dirt bikes and ATVs. "We'll meet Martin at Goat Mountain," Gunderson said, his voice tinged with disbelief. "After all these years, it's hard to grasp that the culmination is so near."

Johns leaned back, withdrawing into himself. He imagined what it might feel like to reunite with Helene and their son, not as separate beings, but as expressions of the same essence. In this new incarnation, he hoped for no more barriers of separation, no more divisions of "us" and "them." The great truth of unity would be ever-present, a constant reminder of the interconnectedness that lay beneath the surface of all things.

He sank deeper into the seat cushions, letting the desert's stillness wash over him as they drove onward.

58

SARAH AND MARTIN

GOAT MOUNTAIN, LANDERS, CALIFORNIA

The sun shone high above the rugged landscape of Goat Mountain as Sarah stepped out of the SUV, the cool desert air brushing against her skin. The heavy silence was only broken by the distant call of a coyote and the crunch of gravel under her boots. Ahead, a man in his early thirties straddled a dirt bike.

Sarah's heart pounded with a mix of anticipation and apprehension. This was the moment she had been preparing for, the culmination of memories not entirely her own. The memories of Betty Davidson, the woman whose soul now intertwined with hers, flooded her mind—memories of love, loss, and an unwavering bond with the child she had left behind.

Martin was tall, with the same piercing gray eyes Sarah had seen in her memories, eyes that now studied her with a mixture of curiosity and something deeper—an unspoken recognition.

They stood a few feet apart, the space between them filled with the weight of unspoken truths and a lifetime of separation. Martin's voice broke the silence, roughened by years of sadness.

"You're Sarah," he said, more a statement than a question, but his eyes searched hers, seeking something familiar.

Sarah nodded, her voice catching in her throat. "Yes. But also...

Betty. It's like memories of a common lineage we both share going back into deep time. In some ways, it's beyond explanation."

The reality behind her words hung in the air between them, heavy with significance. Martin's expression faltered for a moment, as if he had been struck by an invisible force. He took a slow, deliberate step forward, his eyes never leaving hers.

"Mother..." he whispered, the word barely audible, but laden with emotion. His gaze softened, filled with the echoes of a past life. "All these years, I thought I would never see you again."

Tears pricked at the corners of Sarah's eyes, but she held them back, taking a steadying breath. "I'm here, Martin. Different, but the same. I came back ... for this."

Martin's hand trembled as he reached out, hesitating before his fingers brushed against her arm. "I understand now."

She placed her hand over his, grounding them both in the reality of the moment. Now fully Sarah again, she said, "There's something we need to finish."

He smiled. "We have a mountain to climb."

Gunderson watched the intimate moment with an intensity that went beyond simple curiosity. The integration of Betty's memories had been seamless. For the first time since the merging of the Prometheus and Anodos Explorer projects, he felt real hope they would succeed. He coughed, and the reunion between mother and son ended. "You have the bioelectric stimulator?"

Martin patted the backpack leaning against the motorcycle. From the bike's second pannier, he pulled out another pack sloshing with the water stored inside. He handed the pack to Gunderson. He led the three of them around the massive boulder to the trail leading up Goat Mountain. Not another word was said.

59

A STUNNING REVELATION

GOAT MOUNTAIN

The fast-moving clouds obscured the sun as Martin led the group up the mountain's steep, rocky incline. The climb was grueling, especially for Johns, who desperate for water and food lagged behind, the weight of the backpack carrying the Eye pressing him down with each step. Martin moved with purpose, his eyes fixed on the peak, while Gunderson, ever the steady presence, followed closely behind. Sarah stayed with Johns, her eyes flicking between the path ahead and his faltering steps while offering words of encouragement and a steady hand whenever he stumbled.

Near the top, the wind picked up, and dust and sand swirled around them in a chaotic dance. A hundred feet below the summit, Martin paused. Motioning to Gunderson, they pulled back a large stone, revealing the dark opening to an old mine. The entrance, hidden, now stood before them like a gateway to another world.

John's breath came in ragged gasps as he and Sarah reached the mine. The wind raged around them, stirring up fine particles that made the air hard to breathe. Gunderson and Martin waved them inside, but Johns hesitated, the climb and the dark entrance daunting.

Sarah placed a hand on his arm. "There's no turning back now," she yelled above the storm. Hands reached out and dragged them inside.

Inside the cramped space the air was cool and still, a stark contrast to the chaos outside. Martin flashed a Maglite on the walls, illuminating the Greek symbols. "We're here," he told the others.

Martin checked his watch. Since the activation of the Explorer would not take place until at least an hour after launch, they had plenty of time and did not have to rush. While Gunderson and Sarah deployed an inflatable mattress on the ground, he checked Johns' vital signs. "You're in good shape, Isaac," he said, correctly interpreting Johns' look of concern.

"I feel like shit," Johns confessed.

Martin sighed. "You'll do fine."

With Sarah's help, Martin gently eased John onto the mattress. Gunderson took the backpack from Johns, his hands moving with practiced precision as he pulled out the object they had come so far to use—the Eye.

The ancient artifact gleamed in the meager light streaming through a narrow slit from above. Shadows flickered around them.

Gunderson practiced the chant, his voice deep and resonant, the sound of "e, i, o, y" echoing through the space, filling it with an otherworldly energy. The vibrations seeped into the very walls, which would amplify the power of the ritual.

With a calm that belied the storm outside, Martin attached the two electrodes from his bioelectric machine to John's temples and chest, his fingers moving deftly over the controls as he initiated the bioelectrical signaling to test that their connection was functioning. The air crackled with a strange energy, and for a moment, time stood still.

Gunderson placed the Eye in John's trembling hands.

Johns stared into its depths. The world around him faded away. His body stiffened, and then, in an instant, he was gone.

"Martin! What the heck?" Sarah shouted, hovering nearby but afraid to touch Johns.

"I didn't do anything—the plan is to put him under before the

Explorer is activated." Martin checked the readout on his device then lifted Johns' eyelids to check his blown pupils.

Gunderson crossed his arms and fingered his chin, pursing his lips. "Interesting."

They waited in tense silence, the minutes stretching on interminably. The storm outside roared louder, as if in anticipation, but inside the mine, only the quiet hum of the machine and the steady rhythm of their breaths broke the silence.

Then, without warning, John convulsed violently, as if struck by a powerful current. The seizure lasted only seconds, but it felt like an eternity to those watching. When it finally subsided, Johns sat up abruptly, his eyes wide and wild, as if he had seen something far beyond their understanding.

"The guide sent me back," he gasped, his voice hoarse and trembling. "With a message... 'Wrong person, wrong place.'"

The words hung in the air, heavy with implications they were not yet ready to face and the unsettling realization their journey was far from over.

60

TRANSFORMATION

GOAT MOUNTAIN

The air in the mine was thick with tension. Johns got up slowly, pushing away hands that would help him and moved into a dark corner of the mine. Sarah stood off to the side, watching as Gunderson and Martin hurriedly gathered up the mat and stowed away the bioelectric stimulator. Their faces, usually marked by a stoic determination, now showed only disbelief.

Martin, his voice barely above a whisper, turned to Gunderson. "What now?" he asked, the words heavy with uncertainty.

Before Gunderson could respond, a movement from the corner drew all eyes. Johns stepped forward, emerging from the shadows' edge like a being reborn into flesh. The others knew instinctively this was not the same Johns who had entered the mine a half-hour ago. No, this man was different—his very essence had shifted. His posture was upright, his steps purposeful, his entire being exuding an electric energy.

He walked with an ease and confidence that stunned the others into silence. This was no longer the hesitant widower uncertain of his place in the world. He was transformed, as if the nonphysical world had imbued him with a power both ancient and all-knowing.

Without a word, Johns reached down and, in one fluid motion, picked up the Eye and slipped it into his backpack. Then, with a calmness that belied the gravity of the moment, he handed the pack to Sarah.

"You're the one," he said, his voice steady, his gaze unwavering.

Sarah's heart pounded in her chest. She took the backpack from him, her hands trembling. The weight of the Eye felt different now, heavier, as if it recognized its true bearer. Disbelief flickered in her eyes, mingling with awe as the truth settled over her like a blessing from God. Betty had orchestrated everything since the beginning of the Prometheus Project, leading to this moment. She was the one—the one who would carry the burden, the one who would fulfill the realization of humanity's next step.

Johns' voice, now commanding and resolute, cut through the silence. "By the time we reach the bottom of this mountain, you will know where to go." The finality of his words instilled confidence in the others.

Whatever doubts lingered in Sarah's mind were swept away, replaced by a fierce determination. She nodded, the last vestiges of uncertainty melting away. Gunderson embraced Johns tightly, whispering words only he could hear. "You are one of us now. The torch has been passed."

Johns returned the embrace, a silent acknowledgment of the profound change that had taken place within him because of the near-death experience. Then, with a final glance at the group, he turned and strode confidently into the storm raging outside the mine. The swirling sand and wind parted before him as if recognizing the power he now wielded.

61

AMBUSH

GOAT MOUNTAIN

The sandstorm howled with an otherworldly fury; a force of nature bent on erasing their presence from the mountain. It was as if the very earth sought to expel them, pushing them toward the barren desert below. The wind screamed, swirling sands obscuring the world beyond their small circle of vision, and each step became a battle against an unseen adversary.

"If Goat Mountain wasn't the right place, then where do we go?" Martin shouted above the howling wind. His voice was strained, laden with worry, his heart heavy with the weight of uncertainty. The launch had taken place and the window for success was rapidly closing.

Johns, his expression inscrutable, spoke with an eerie calmness, "Sarah knows."

Sarah, her eyes alight with an unspoken knowledge, lifted her gaze from the glowing screen of her phone. "It's the Integratron," she murmured, her voice small in the roaring wind. "I have a signal. I need to make a call."

Martin looked at her, his confusion deepening, unsure if he was gazing at the young woman before him or the ghost of his mother. "How do you know?" he asked, his voice tinged with desperation.

A cryptic smile played on Sarah's lips. "I'll tell you later," she replied. Without another word, she brought the phone to her ear, her voice steady as she spoke, "This is Simon Ravensbach's daughter."

She listened intently, the silence stretching on for what felt like an eternity, before nodding to herself. "We'll meet you there as soon as we can," she said, the words carrying an unspoken urgency.

Martin glanced at his watch, the ticking seconds a reminder of the relentless march of time. "It had better be nearby. Our window of opportunity is closing fast."

"We'll make it," Sarah assured him.

Johns led the way as the four of them broke into a determined trot, the storm at their backs, racing against time and fate toward whatever destiny awaited them.

As the group reached the base of the mountain, the air reverberated with a tension that mirrored the storm they had just escaped. Johns, a hundred yards ahead, rounded the massive boulder that obscured the trailhead from the vast desert. His heart skipped a beat when he spotted a strange Range Rover parked beside their SUV.

Before he could warn the others, a deep, commanding voice rang out, "Dr. Johns, please don't make any trouble for yourself or your friends."

From the shadow of the cars, a towering figure emerged. In his left hand, Beast held a Glock-19 with an ease that belied its deadly potential. Beside him stood a young man, his frame lean and wiry, exuding a quiet, predatory grace. The way he moved, feline and fluid, sent alarms through Johns' mind. Beast gestured for Johns to come forward, positioning him so he had a clear view of the others when they arrived.

"Search him," Beast ordered.

The young man stepped forward, his movements precise as he patted Johns down, finding nothing of interest. He returned to Beast's side, eyes alert.

"What now?" Johns asked, his voice calm but his mind racing.

"We wait for your friends," Beast replied, his tone cold.

Johns glanced at the young man. "Who's your friend?"

"Janus Snyder," the young man answered, his voice devoid of emotion.

Recognition flickered in Johns' eyes. "I know you... from Sedona. You were sent to kill us."

"I didn't, though," Snyder replied, a trace of something unreadable in his gaze.

"Not for lack of trying," Johns retorted, his eyes narrowing. "You're here for the Eye."

Snyder nodded, his silence an acknowledgment of the truth. "Where is it?"

There was no point in lying; in mere moments, Sarah and the others would walk into the trap. "It's coming," he said, resigned.

The scrape of shoes on the dry rocky path reached them, and seconds later, Gunderson, Sarah, and Martin emerged from behind the boulder, their eyes widening as they took in the scene.

They froze, seeing Beast with the gun aimed at them, raising hands instinctively in surrender. Gunderson's eyes darted to the boulder, gauging the distance, calculating their slim chances.

"Gunderson," Beast said smoothly, his voice a silken threat. "You know I am an initiate and an adept. Please, don't do anything foolish."

Snyder and Beast herded the group into the narrow space between the cars, away from the wind and escape.

"What do you want?" Gunderson asked, his voice steady despite the thick tension.

"The bioelectric stimulator, of course, and the Eye," Beast answered, his tone laced with greed.

"Cynthia and Sam Hill sent you for them, didn't they?" Gunderson pressed.

Beast laughed, a harsh, grating sound in the sere heat. "They are fools. I'm taking both for myself."

"Of course," Martin said, his voice edged with sarcasm. "The technology would be invaluable to anyone craving power."

Snyder's eyebrows arched slightly at this, but he remained silent, his focus shifting to Sarah. She seemed different now, more mature, more composed, than the young woman who had lost her father nine months ago. He thought of Simon Ravensbach, the man he had killed, and his rebellion against his parents and the Prometheus Project. Part of him silently wanted her to give up the Eye and for the Marine doctor to hand over the bioelectric stimulator without a fight.

"We weren't successful," Gunderson said. "We have to go to a different place, or the Anodos Explorer Project will fail."

"Not my concern." Beast leveled the Glock at Martin and Sarah. "Give me the bioelectric stimulator and the Eye, or I'll shoot you all and take them anyway."

Sarah frowned, a spark of defiance in her eyes. "You're a fool. You have no future."

Beast's gaze hardened, his finger tightening on the trigger. "I can see things you don't."

"Wait, there's no hurry," Martin interjected quickly. "Let us complete our mission, and we'll give you both gladly."

"I'm tired of waiting," Beast growled, motioning with the pistol. "Janus, get the backpacks. We're leaving."

Snyder had been listening intently, every sense heightened by his Gnostic training. Tension radiated from Beast, the man's mind already set on killing them all. The only reason he hadn't pulled the trigger yet was the fear of damaging the artifacts. The *xiphos*, Snyder's short Greek sword, was within easy reach, but any sudden move would likely get him shot.

Gunderson's hands dropped to his sides. "No," he said, and in the same instant, he launched himself at Beast. His movements were supernaturally agile, too fast to follow. But Beast, an adept in his own right, sidestepped smoothly and fired twice. Gunderson's body jerked violently and collapsed in a lifeless heap.

The motion placed Beast dangerously close to Snyder. Without hesitation, Snyder chopped Beast's wrist, sending the gun skidding under the Range Rover. Momentarily stunned by the sudden reversal, Beast reacted with the speed of a seasoned warrior. He drove a powerful heel palm strike into Snyder's chest, sending him crashing into the SUV. As if by magic, a knife appeared in Beast's other hand.

He lunged forward, but Snyder, moving with the grace of a dancer, spun out of the way. The blade clanged off the hood of the vehicle.

In the same fluid motion, Snyder brought his *xiphos* to bear, the blade gleaming in the harsh sunlight. The two men squared off, their movements slow, deliberate, each step a deadly dance of life and death, their blades flashing as they tested each other's defenses.

"Go!" Snyder shouted, his voice cutting through the tension.

Johns' legs felt like lead, his mind paralyzed as he stared at Gunderson's lifeless body lying in a pool of blood. Hands grabbed him, pulling him back to reality. "In the car!" Sarah yelled, shoving him toward the passenger door. The SUV roared to life, tires spinning wildly in the loose sand.

"We can't leave Gerald!" Johns shouted, trying to push past Martin to get to the door.

Martin's hands clamped down on his arms, forcing him back into the seat. "He's gone, Isaac. I'm sorry."

Sarah drove fast, the SUV fishtailing until she found a hardened dirt track and sped along it. Her eyes flicked to the rearview mirror. Dust and distance obscured the brutal fight behind them, but Snyder's voice echoed in her mind, chilling her with the memory of who he was—the man who had killed her father. A part of her wanted to turn around, to take her revenge.

Betty's voice whispered in her mind, *"Anodos Explorer needs you. It is the culmination of your father's and your life's work."*

She was right. The mission was more important than vengeance. Sarah tightened her grip on the wheel, her resolve hardening.

"The Integratron is only minutes away," Sarah said, her voice steely with determination.

62

THE INTEGRATRON
LANDERS, CALIFORNIA

The barren expanse of the Mojave Desert embraced them as they reached the empty parking lot of the dome-shaped Integratron. The structure loomed with an aura both inviting and forbidding. A mystical silence hung in the air.

Sarah's eyes locked onto a tall, spare woman standing in the doorway, her figure a silhouette against the dim light spilling from within. Martin and John exchanged anxious glances, their hearts heavy with the weight of what was to come. Every step Sarah took toward the building felt measured, as if the earth itself was holding its breath.

"Nancy," Sarah said, her voice heavy with relief.

The older woman opened her arms, and the two women embraced, a union of past and present, a momentary reprieve from the growing tension. Nancy's voice, gentle yet laden with meaning, broke the heartfelt silence. "You are a strong, stalwart woman, Sarah. Your father has prepared you and us for this moment."

Sarah nodded. "I understand why he took me here now."

"We haven't much time." Nancy's gaze took in all of them. "Come inside. My sister, Joy, is preparing the way."

Inside the dome, the air was thick with anticipation. Joy moved with purpose, her hands preparing a sacred space in the center of the room.

John and Martin entered the dome, their minds racing at the scene before them. Sarah lay on a bed, candles flickering softly around her, casting shadows that danced with the light. Five quartz crystal-song bowls stood sentinel, their silent presence a promise of what was to come.

The structure's precise geometry amplified the energy swirling within. An invisible force pulsed with the rhythm of their anxious hearts. The beauty of the place and its metaphysical significance were overwhelming.

Nancy said with reverence, "George Van Tassel was told to build this structure for this purpose. It stands at the intersection of two of the most powerful energetic ley lines."

Sarah's breath remained steady yet heavy with the weight of the moment. Johns handed her the Eye; her fingertips turned white where they gripped the ancient tile resting on her chest. Martin, moving with practiced skill, attached electrodes to her body, each connection amplifying the anticipation.

Johns began the chant, his voice deep and resonant as he intoned the primeval vowels. The acoustics of the dome amplified every tone. The others joined in, their voices melding into a singular sound that filled the space. The air vibrated with their voices, causing the singing bowls to resonate on their own. The entire building came alive, vibrating with an intensity that echoed through their very beings. In that moment, they all became one with the acoustics of the place, the sound waves carrying them beyond the physical realm.

At the height of the radiant energy, Martin initiated the bioelectrical pattern.

Sarah's body tensed. Her breathing became shallow until no air passed into her lungs.

Watching carefully, Johns waited for any sign the process was working. Sarah's hands slipped from the Eye, a silent admission to the power of the energy in the building. Martin, with trembling fingers, carefully disconnected the electrodes and removed them.

They waited, the minutes stretching into eternity, each one filled with anxious dread as the bowls continued their haunting song.

Suddenly, the singing bowls faded to quiet. Silence fell like a shroud, heavy and suffocating.

Martin moved instinctively to begin chest compressions, but Johns placed a gentle hand on his shoulder, stopping him.

"The next world is beyond anything we can comprehend," Johns murmured, his voice thick with emotion. "Words can't capture its beauty or mystery. Sarah is okay, more than okay."

Martin swallowed, struggling to accept the truth. "To imagine a life beyond senses, beyond sight, sound, smell, or touch...it's unthinkable."

"Whatever she's experiencing now, it's not an end but a beginning—one wrapped in love, beyond any of our words or feelings."

A single tear slipped down Martin's cheek as Johns nodded, sharing his pain and grief.

From across the room, Joy's voice trembled as she broke the silence. "I've called 911."

Yet as the truth settled within him, something entirely new bloomed within Martin—a glimmer of hope, bright and unwavering. The Anodos Project, Sarah's life, had been a beacon, guiding humanity toward something greater. For the first time, he knew they would succeed.

Martin, his voice soft but resolute, said, "Isaac is right. My mother is exactly where she needs to be."

Johns thought, *There is so much work to be done yet. I have the truth of Eleusis to bring to the world.*

EPILOGUE

Sarah's death was attributed to hypertrophic cardiomyopathy (HCM), a genetic heart condition characterized by abnormal thickening of the heart muscle, which can disrupt the heart's electrical system and lead to arrhythmias that can cause sudden cardiac arrest. Donations in her name may be made to the Key to My Heart Foundation in honor of her dedication to the sport of gymnastics in her youth.

Thirteen hours after the Anodos Explorer was activated, flight controllers at Vandenberg Space Force Base lost contact with the Von Neumann Universal Constructor, as planned. In that moment, General Deke Davidson knew that the Prometheus project was a success.

Subsequent to the launch, he retired from the Space Force and joined Boeing's Aerospace Division to work on antigravity propulsion. He can often be spotted at Rose Hills Memorial Park in Whittier, California, visiting the gravesites of Sarah Davenport and his wife, Betty. The cemetery lies not far from the Buddha pagoda where the general stops to meditate.

The Eye is currently on temporary loan to Yale's Peabody Museum. The exhibit states the votive stone is an exact replica of the

Eye displayed in the Athens Museum. However, many visitors who stare at the Eye report altered state experiences.

Professor Isaac Johns returned to Yale for the spring semester. At a cocktail party, he met a woman who is a professor in the physics department, and who is also a mutant. They launched a laboratory aimed at creating a new physics based on near-death experiences and plan to marry in the fall on the anniversary of Isaac's awakening as an initiate. His wife had communicated in the nonphysical realm that this is what he should do.

Zach Helm spent two months recovering in the Edward G. Hirschman Regional Burn Center in Riverside, California. Returning to his parents' home in Sioux City, Iowa, he continued his recovery while working on *The Eleusinian Mysteries* documentary, using footage on the hard drive that Johns sent to him. The documentary is expected to premier on streaming within the year.

William Gallagher, the Dominican Friar Augustus, gave up his efforts to obtain the Eye. He conveyed the Scroll to the Vatican, where the third century BCE document was sequestered in the *Archivum Apostolicum Vaticanum*, a secret central repository. He is now in charge of a Papal task force to determine a plausible explanation for the fact that people who have near-death experiences never report visiting hell.

On his way to the Integratron, Major Martin Davidson texted members of the Invisibles Academy at Edwards Air Force Base. Using a stealth hypersonic experimental vehicle, they were able to retrieve the bodies of Beast, Snyder, and Gunderson and take them to their secret lab for brain analysis to see if new structures had developed and were passed on to a second-generation mutant. Major Davidson has rededicated his career to using the bioelectrical stimulator to cure cancer.

Cynthia Apple and Sam Hill believe it is only a matter of time before their allies will be able to reverse-engineer the bioelectrical stimulator, opening the way for expanding the Academy and pushing the merging of technology and humans into a singularity.

ABOUT THE AUTHORS

Ronald Meyer is a seasoned paranormal experiencer, with encounters ranging from out-of-body experiences and cryptid sightings to non-dual awakenings. He is the owner of Centre Communications, a film production company, and has produced and directed feature films in Hollywood. Ron also facilitates flow workshops and holds a 5th-degree black belt in Aikido. Recently, he produced *Becoming Evil*, the number one streaming documentary series on Amazon Prime about serial killers. Additionally, he is a peer-reviewed published scientist with contributions to the fields of behavioral cybernetics and paleontology. He resides in Louisville, Colorado, with his wife.

In September 2023, Centre Communications premiered the feature film *The Mysteries of Bradshaw Ranch: Aliens, Portals, and the Paranormal* at a conference in Vernal, adjacent to Skinwalker Ranch. During the movie's production, the crew encountered intelligent alien entities and other paranormal phenomena. The film is slated for release in early 2024.

Mark Reeder writes science fiction and fantasy for both adults and young adults, and is the author of the Jack Doyle paranormal detective series. He's kicked around the universe long enough to have more than a few bumps and bruises. Roughed up and battered like his hat, he's still looking for the exit.

AFTERWORD

Go to hangarıpublishing.com to learn more about the Authors and stay up to date with their newest releases.

www.ingramcontent.com/pod-product-compliance
Lightning Source LLC
Chambersburg PA
CBHW060310310726
48976CB00007B/2272

Two thousand years ago, in a hidden cave near Jerusalem, something extraordinary happened—an event so profound it would remain secret until now.

Present day: When Sarah Davenport witnesses her father's murder, his dying words leave her with a sequence of numbers and a mystery that will challenge everything she believes about human consciousness, technology, and the very nature of reality.

Yale professor Isaac Johns has spent his career studying the Eleusinian Mysteries of ancient Greece, never expecting to find himself thrust into one. But when Sarah appears with an artifact that shouldn't exist and a story that sounds impossible, he's forced to question everything he knows about history, science, and the thin line between life and death.

As powerful forces converge around them—the Catholic Church, Silicon Valley visionaries, and shadowy figures willing to kill to protect ancient secrets—Sarah and Johns race to unlock a truth that could change humanity forever. Their journey will take them from the hidden caves of Sedona to the cutting-edge laboratories of the modern space program, where the impossible becomes possible and the line between science and mysticism disappears.

Meyer and Reeder masterfully weave historical mystery with bleeding-edge science in this visionary thriller that will leave you questioning everything you thought you knew about consciousness, technology, and the human soul. What if humanity's next great leap forward isn't about advancing our bodies, but transcending them entirely?

Perfect for fans of Dan Brown, Michael Crichton, and James Rollins, this genre-defying novel will challenge your beliefs and keep you guessing until the final page.

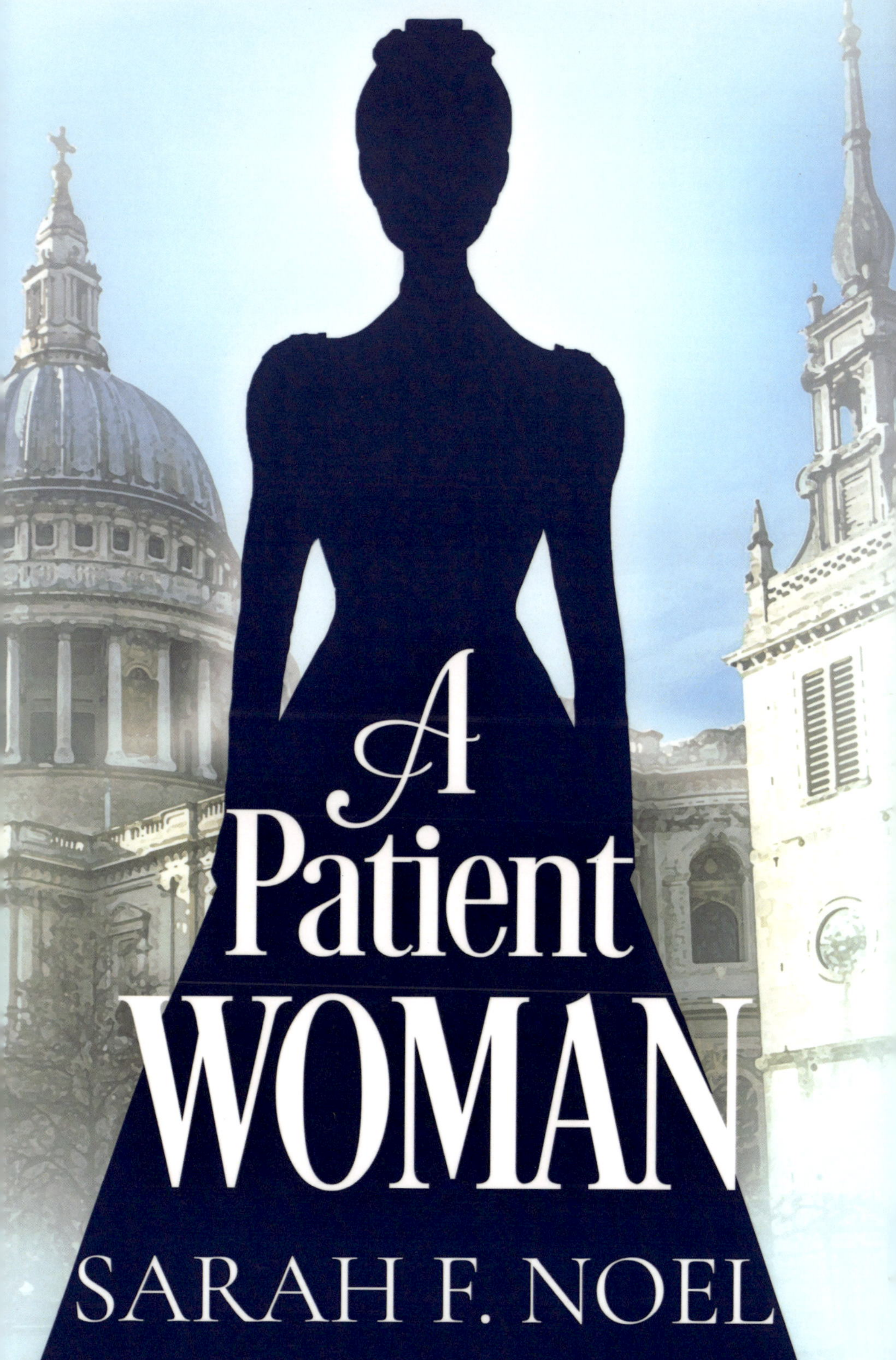

A TABITHA & WOLF MYSTERY
A
Patient
WOMAN
SARAH F. NOEL